The Sound of Water

The Sound of Water

A Novel

Sanjay Bahadur

ATRIA INTERNATIONAL
New York London Toronto Sydney

ATRIA INTERNATIONAL
A Division of Simon & Schuster, Inc.
1230 Avenue of the Americas
New York, NY 10020

First Atria International trade paperback edition June 2009

ATRIA INTERNATIONAL and colophon are trademarks of Simon & Schuster, Inc.

For information about special discounts for bulk purchases,
please contact Simon & Schuster Special Sales at
1-866-506-1949 or business@simonandschuster.com.

The Simon & Schuster Speakers Bureau can bring authors
to your live event. For more information or to book an event,
contact the Simon & Schuster Speakers Bureau at
1-866-248-3049 or visit our website at www.simonspeakers.com.

Designed by Davina Mock-Maniscalco

Manufactured in the United States of America

10 9 8 7 6 5 4 3 2 1

Library of Congress Cataloging-in-Publication Data

Bahadur, Sanjay.
   The sound of water : a novel / Sanjay Bahadur.
p. cm.
1. Coal mines and mining—India—Fiction. 2. Coal mine accidents—Psychological aspects—
Fiction. 3. India—Fiction. 4. Domestic fiction. 5. Psychological fiction. I. Title.
   PR9499.2.B34S58 2009
   823'.92—dc22   2008040499

ISBN 978-1-4165-8569-5
ISBN 978-1-4165-8590-9 (ebook)

In memory of Fateh Jung Bahadur,
officer, gentleman, thinker, book lover,
and
my father

There was neither non-existence nor existence then:
There was no realm of air, no sky beyond it.
What covered in, and where? and what gave shelter?
    Was water there, unfathomed depth of water?
Death was not then, nor was there aught immortal:
    no sign was there, the day's and night's divider.
That One Thing, breathless, breathed by its own
    nature: apart from it was nothing whatsoever.
Darkness there was: at first concealed in darkness.
    This all was watery chaos.
All that existed then was void and formless: by the great
    power of Warmth was born that Unit.

—From the *Nasadiya Sukta* of Rig Veda
(Hymn 129 of the tenth Mandala)
Based on translation by Ralph T. H. Griffith,
The Hymns of the Rig Veda, 2nd edition, Kotagiri, Nilgiri,
1896

If there were water

And no rock

If there were rock

And also water

And water

A spring

A pool among the rock

If there were the sound of water only

Not the cicada

And dry grass singing

But sound of water over a rock

Where the hermit-thrush sings in the pine trees

Drip drop drip drop drop drop drop

But there is no water

—T. S. Eliot, *The Waste Land*

chapter 1

It is comfortable in the tombdark womb of the earth. Two hundred and fifty feet beneath the arid crust, it is quiet and cool—the charcoal silence broken only by the faint rustle of water slithering down the flakywhite walls and pitchdark ceiling. Raimoti pauses to listen. Nothing. He has strayed a little distance away from his gang of six coal diggers enjoying their well-earned dinner break at the coal face. Raimoti strains his ears, craning his wrinkled neck to catch the faintest whisper. He is seeking the sound of water: not the harmless pearl-drop tinkle but the deathly murmur of little waves lapping against the lean barrier of rocks. Today there is just the dry stone, no water. Only shadow under the black rock.

For almost a century, his father and his father's father before that—all miners—had lived dreading the sound and died in peace. For close to forty years Raimoti has continued their quest, but the Beast still eludes him. He hopes only to die like his forefathers on the surface, in a dry bed. He fears the Beast and wants to hunt it down before it hunts him out. He fears death by water. He fears being immersed and immured for eternity, within the dark labyrinth beneath the earth where even his gods wouldn't look for him. But he is a brave man, and so he hunts.

He doesn't look like much of a hunter as he crouches, worried, on the mine floor. He has a face that is of indeterminate age but is of someone no longer young. A web of deep wrinkles trickles down from his bony forehead and runs as lost rivulets across his crusty skin and along the corners of his mouth, collecting in shadowy puddles around his protuberant eyes and the hollows of his cheeks. His thinning hair is more gray than black and stands in erratic spirals on an elongated head, giving him a slightly startled look. Reality surprises Raimoti. And his eyes carry a wonderment that comes from questioning the sun and accepting the moon. From doubting light and believing in shadows.

No one, not even his long-dead mother, has ever found Raimoti handsome, but his face has a certain charm that frankness and simplicity bestow on people with uncomplicated hearts. Crooked, tobacco-stained teeth jostling behind his lips add to his bemused expression and are often responsible for luring people into believing that he can be pushed. His crumpled, large ears are a prominent feature of his face. They jut out from the sides of his head as he swivels them in his surreptitious quest for sounds: flat sounds, sharp sounds, dry sounds, wet sounds, colored sounds, white sounds. Black sounds. Sounds within. And from the world outside. His ears soak them all up and interfere with his heartbeats.

Raimoti peers dimly through the shadows and leans closer

to the walls of the mine. His long and rough hands grope at the bumpy surface of the tunnel, feeling its coolness. He wipes some dust off with the tips of his fingers and sniffs at it with quivering nostrils. Sometimes soul can hide inside the body, but uttered words can reveal its nature. Sometimes water can hide inside dull rocks but is betrayed by restless dirt that can carry scents. But today the coal dust is sullen and silent—resisting questions, yielding no secrets. At times earth can be unresponsive like this.

He turns on his heels and squats on his haunches, leaning his tired back against the wall, his thin forearms resting on his knees. Working underground is hard on the body and harder on the mind. It rapidly eats away youth, drains energy, and corrodes thoughts. In some worlds, a man may reach his prime after half a century of existence, but in this one at that age, the only thing that remains is a man's spirit—and often not even that. Raimoti sighs. He feels too old but has some fight left in him yet. All his life, winning hasn't mattered, because he has been saving himself up for the one confrontation that he knows he is destined to have. He knows it will happen. He just doesn't know how soon.

He turns his head to one side—away from the light. For a moment he thinks that he caught a glimpse of a sudden movement. After a few seconds, he lets out his breath, realizing that he held it for too long. He stands up slowly and arches his back to get rid of the dull ache that never seems to leave him nowadays. It wasn't so in his youth. He turns to take a look at the far end of the tunnel and decides there is time for a little more exploration.

As he enters deeper darkness, Raimoti clicks on his headlamp. A pale wisp of light emerges and wafts ahead of him, creating shapes that need interpreting, and throws lifelessness into sharp relief: pilings, rivets, roof wedges, rusted rails, debris of abandoned implements, and of course, unpredictable boulders of coal. They grow wild in the mines.

None of these is going to talk to him. He has to find his own answers. The deeper he goes, the more solid the shadows around him become. Silence creeps in from all sides and screams around his ears, making him even more edgy. Only his nose unearths a new fact: a faint smell of death that wasn't there till yesterday. He has known for long that the rocks in this part of the mine are ailing. They do not have long to live. But he had not expected that the end would come so soon or so suddenly. In here there is too little hope to feed them, and almost no happiness, and coal is delicate and vulnerable to melancholia, which abounds in this mine.

Raimoti believes in exhausting all possibilities before giving up, so over the last few weeks, he tried to talk about it to the supervisor and warn him, but no one pays much attention to what he says these days. Dejected, he tried to get assigned to another mine, but the manager did not want to talk to him. This mine and the men working in it are different. Men are not assigned to this mine. They are condemned to work here.

Anyone entering this mine can sense a life-sapping shroud falling over his mind, sucking out positive thoughts and suffocating aspirations. The men working in here are all hand-picked by the company for special treatment. Every day these fading men wear their faded blues and reluctantly descend into the unrelenting depths of this mine—running away from the despairing emptiness of their lives above and toward the anesthetic hardness of coal below. Inside, they drill, hammer, dig, scrape, heave, and haul. They do things to unresisting rocks that they cannot do to people they leave behind on the surface. They exhaust themselves so that when they return to the world above, they carry less weight on their minds. Over time, some start losing bits of their souls to the underground. They deal with this by drinking. They drink hard so they can go down the next day, and then they drink harder after surviving one more day underground. They drink because they are lost on the surface, and they drink because they cannot find peace underground. This is not a place to exist. And it is a worse place to die.

Mine Number 3 is the oldest operational mine in the Area, dug open about a decade ago. It is quiet down here because the mine has been nearly abandoned. The machines are all gone. The drills, the trolleys, the fancy side-dumping loaders have long been shifted to the newest coal seam opened by the company. Even most of the men have gone. Only a handful of miners and foremen remain to work in the remotest corners, the darkest alleys, and the least accessible crevices of the mine, to extract the last pound of flesh from the earth. The clever young engineers have fine-carved the pillars to the last possible millimeter of the statutory twenty meters, in the hopes of maximizing the corporate goal of optimum offtake or production volume. The face has been taken to the extremes, leaving just a few holes where they want to extract a few more tons of the mineral. For this, they have deployed the "least productive" miners and supervisors: those too old or too young to be useful in the newer mines. There are also some known trouble-makers—insubordinate men who have dared think of themselves as equals of the charmed executives, yet who have continued to stay unaffiliated with the labor unions. They are all dregs. Expendable.

Raimoti is aware of this. He has lived all his life in coal mines. He knows how things work here, below the surface, away from the prying eyes of humanity. In his life, he has replaced many a miner lost to age, injury, or death. He has learned to accept the inevitable. In this dark and remorseless world, there are no winners or losers. There are only survivors. At first the machines were to aid men; now men toil to serve the machines. He knows that in a few months, as soon as he attains the officially acknowledged age of fifty-five, he will quietly be asked by the company to opt for voluntary retirement. He is nearing the end of the tunnel. He doesn't mind that—he knows that the company has been fooled, just as his father intended. At least he will see daylight for the rest of his days.

Raimoti stops walking when he reaches an intersection. He realizes that the light from his headlamp is adding nothing to his vision, so he turns it off and stands still with his eyes shut, trying to see what eyes cannot reveal. The veil of darkness first breaks into narrow strips and then disintegrates into strands, allowing concentric circles of radiance to wash over him in ripples. He abandons himself to the warmth of that glow and drifts through space, time, and memories. He does this often. It soothes him as his mind floats across the surrounding harshness of life toward the seductive sponginess of nostalgia. Slowly, the pervading stench of dying rocks gives way to a fertile fragrance of wishful thoughts.

He is a small child nestled against the comfort of his mother's breasts. He cannot make out her face, but he can feel the love behind her smile and hear the soft murmurings of affection in his big ears. She smells of moist earth after the first showers of the monsoon. When he is a little older and they walk on dewy grass while she holds his fingers, he can feel the hidden pulse in her palm. It is all so real that he begins to believe it must have been true. He believes that at some point in life, he must have been truly loved—that he was happy.

Another strand of darkness snaps, and he is sprinting through paddy fields chasing a giant who must be his father. The giant looks back and waits for the little boy to catch up. Raimoti feels a thrill as his father lifts him clear off the green ground and places him on wide shoulders. He feels the flutters of flying birds and the moist caress of the clouds in heaven as he straddles his father's back, his head touching the blue sky. God! He thinks. Can there be a greater joy?

Under the mining helmet, Raimoti's face acquires the hint of a smile. He squeezes his eyelids together with greater determination, hoping to force some more flowers out of a dead ground.

This time he is a young boy sitting under a tamarind tree, listening with rapt attention to a man singing to a god. The boy feels a bubble riding up his throat and bursting from his open lips.

In that silent corridor, Raimoti's voice rings out loud and bounces off the rocks. He knows it can't reach the heavens, but still, it pleases him. He sings out another line and waits for the ricochet. It doesn't come. He sings another line—this time more softly, warily, afraid to disturb the impassive stones. But the walls are unresponsive. He nods knowingly: Today they are hiding something, and he has a fair idea what. He sings no more but concentrates on the glow on the inside of his eyelids.

The flashes of light rearrange to form a young man making love to a woman. Again, he can create no faces but can feel the frenzied breathing and hear the moans. Her body is supple and receptive and matches each thrust with equal passion. In time, the man rolls off, breathing heavily. The woman tries to pull him back and, finding him inert, tries to straddle him. But the man is completely spent. The lights become angryred and intense and contract to two circles that are head-lights of a monster truck. The woman glances back toward the young man, then merges into the silhouette of the truck as it roars off. The man watches helplessly. Raimoti relives the man's perplexed agony.

His eyes, though still closed, smart with a forgotten pain, and everything blurs for a moment. And in that blur he thinks he sees an-other woman floating out of the shimmering haze. This time he cannot make out the size or shape of her body. She seems to be made of flames, and he feels the burn. He watches inwardly as the two figures dance a rhythmless dance from one corner of his eyes to another, fusing and slowly curling into ashes.

Nothing happens for a while, and then a black wooden doll emerges from the ashes and stares fixedly at him. Something stirs at its feet, and Raimoti is surprised to see the young man reappear from the ashes. He seems calm, almost detached. The doll slides toward him, but every time she comes close, the man takes a step away. At last the man halts outside the entrance of a cave, and the doll stops following. He takes a long, hard look at it and leaps into the gaping mouth of the cave.

Inside the gloomy cavern, the man is blinded. He gropes desper-ately and tries to find his way around the winding passages. He doesn't want to be there but is unable to find his way out. As he cannot see, he learns to follow sounds. Sometimes, when it is too quiet, he sings to dispel silence. Time passes, and he grows gnarled and bent, eventually taking to walking on all fours. His body becomes shaggy and heavy, and he loses his ability to sing. When he tries, it sounds more like a growl. His nails harden and lengthen into claws, and he moves silently through the cave, hunting rodents, snakes, and other small animals.

It is so dark now that Raimoti can barely discern the features of the strange creature that was once a sturdy young man. He tries to get closer to the dim form, but it hears him and lopes off. Raimoti gives a brisk chase, turns a corner, and stops. Ahead is a black lake, and the creature is hunched on the edge. He glares back at Raimoti and swiftly slips into the still waters. There are no ripples. Raimoti moves cautiously to the edge and peers down. He sees his own reflection leering at him. Suddenly, the level of the lake rises so rapidly that he leaps back. The cavern echoes with manic laughter, and a watery shape gushes out to lunge at him.

Raimoti screams and opens his eyes with a shudder. He is perspiring heavily from the play of lights inside his head. There is a very faint chuckle from somewhere deep in the tunnels, and his skin crawls. He looks down at his hands, shaking violently, and curses his wretched life.

He never wanted to be a miner. His father had been a prolific man, producing nine sons and five daughters with his two wives. Only three sons and four daughters survived to adulthood. In his carefree adolescence, Raimoti wanted to be a musician. He had a noble voice, a gift from the gods, and a fine ear for sound. He was always in great demand for *Durga Puja* and *Ramlila*. Once he had also traveled to the state capital for a performance. But everything changed when he lost three of his brothers within a span of two years. With many sisters of marriageable age, his family needed income. His younger brother died suddenly of cholera, just before his eighteenth birthday. So providence provided Raimoti's father a welcome opportunity to bring his wayward son back into the family profession. Raimoti was well above the average age when miners joined the company, so his father bribed the *patwari* to fudge the records and declare Raimoti the younger brother. The memories of his dead brother were buried beneath the immediacy of economic necessity. One fine day Raimoti wrapped his beat-up harmonium in a tattered sheet and picked up the shovel. And although he had lived another man's life all these years, he was determined to die his own death—singing to his gods on a *chaupal* in front of his favorite temple. In the meantime, he hunted for the sound of water, a sound that his father had talked of but never heard; a sound that his grandfather had rambled about in delirium on his deathbed. A sound that spelled doom for a miner.

This morning, after his gang had donned their crumbling gum boots and helmets with torches, Raimoti had a strange foreboding. When they descended the shaft in the wobbly lift and started walking down the murky decline into the labyrinth, he heard the ghost of the Beast stalking them from the flanks. The Beast tiptoed, at times ahead of them, at times behind them, but always around them.

Raimoti feels drained and decides to go no farther. He is sure that he is very close, but he doesn't know where else to search. With heavy treads, he retraces his steps and reaches the place he started.

Raimoti can hear the faint laughter of his mates. He pauses to listen again. Still nothing. He is certain the Beast is lurking somewhere close: stealthy, restless, menacing. He places his hands against the moist walls of the tunnel, painted white with chalk dust as a precaution against accidental combustion of the surface. The rocks palpitate ever so softly, but there is no sound of the footfall of the Beast. As he turns back, he feels the rustle of a thousand fears behind his stooped shoulders. He retreats from the narrow gully into the main corridor, which leads to the mine face where his gang is waiting. He stops to take one last look before the walls squeeze him out to the relative brightness of the dimly lit corridor.

The five of them sit huddled against a small heap of coal that they have extracted. Three barrows have already been filled, and they will work till all six are brimming before they are permitted to return to the surface. Raimoti joins them and squats on his haunches. No one is permitted to smoke in the mine, so they share a slimy pouch of tobacco.

"What's the matter, *kaka*?" Arif asks with a twinkle in his eyes. "Are you hunting again?"

Everyone laughs. They know about Raimoti's eternal quest and find it amusing. Raimoti chews his tobacco in glum silence, spitting out a brownish stream of *pik* on the wall.

"*Arre!* The old man has the jitters again," comments Birsa, a sturdy lad from the hills, barely into his twentieth year. "I tell you, *kaka,* you worry too much, and it gets on our nerves at times. Where did you disappear to?"

"I heard some noises when we were coming down," Raimoti explains patiently, "and I thought I would investigate. I have been worried ever since the lake flooded last week. It is too close to this pit, and we have been digging toward it for the past month. You should be worried, too, *beta*."

"Why? Didn't we have an inspection by the engineers? They declared that the water wall is at least two hundred meters away. We will finish with this corridor by next week, and then they will probably close down the mine and shift us to the new one."

"Hatt re! " Arif says with disdain. "Those *beti-chod sahibs* will never let us leave till a couple of pillars or at least some scaffoldings collapse, breaking a few bones. The *mader-chods* are pitiless. But *kaka,* there really is no reason to fear. We are safe. I heard it from Ram Babu, the supervisor. He has opted for duty while we work this portion so he can take next week off for his daughter's wedding. He is such a coward that he never would have taken the risk if he felt there was the smallest danger."

Arif is the leader of the gang and tends to be abusive and aggressive. He was working in the latest mine, Number 8, when he fell into an argument with a junior engineer and smashed a shovel over the other man's head.

"You tried to break the engineer's head!" the inquiry officer charged.

"No," Arif replied, "I was only trying to break the mother-fucker's teeth. His head got in my way."

Subsequently, Arif also fought with the union representatives who tried to intervene and wrangle some concessions out of the management on the pretext of settling the dispute. Arif called them whores and refused to get involved in their politics. He was promptly shunted to Mine Number 3 to rot. He has known

Raimoti for many years and had been among the first to rush to extract the body of Raimoti's son when he was crushed to death in a minor collapse of the mine ceiling. Since that day Arif, himself an orphan, has loosely adopted Raimoti as a father. This prevents the other youngsters from taking too much liberty with the aging miner. The two also share a love for music and spend hours listening to songs, *quawwalis* and *bhajans,* on Arif's tiny cassette player when Raimoti is sober and not under influence of the locally produced *hadia* or ganja. Arif, a religious man, doesn't consume these *shaitani* poisons. His only weakness is women. He is famed to have slept with every known whore in the vicinity and with some unknown ones besides.

"The only thing I do well is dig," Arif is fond of bragging. "With my pickax and with my prick!"

Raimoti is quite fond of Arif and thinks of him almost as a son. Like his father, Raimoti was a productive man and had six children before *Mahila Jagaran Morcha*—the local women's empowerment group—enlightened his perpetually pregnant wife and she forced him to have a vasectomy. He received an additional increment in recognition of this sacrifice, as per the company's policy. The government wanted its workers to produce more coal, not children. Soon thereafter, his younger son died of tuberculosis, and his older son died in the accident a few years later. His daughters fared better and were alive, to the best of his knowledge, though unhappily married to loaders and miners in other coalfields. He was hardly in touch with them. His wife, Dulari, a comely lady, abandoned him long before for a truck driver, leaving him to look after the children and get them married or cremated, as the situation demanded. Raimoti now lives with his only surviving brother, Madho, the youngest, and Madho's wife and three children. He gives half of whatever he earns to his brother, keeping aside the rest for his addictions and stray personal expenses.

Arif looks at his watch and gets up to stretch. He kisses the pickax and saunters toward the coal face. This is a sign for the others to end their rest. Raimoti, being the oldest and the weakest, is handed the shovel with which he has to keep loading the barrows.

Arif urinates against the exposed boulders of coal, shouting, "Look, *kaka,* I piss into the arsehole of the earth! Now it is plugged from this side—nothing can pass through. You are safe, all you *beti-chods*! Dig away!"

They begin pounding the rock face in a steady rhythm . . . *dha-tun-na! Dha-tun-na! Dha-tun-na!*

They are transported from the reality of the world outside—its sights, its smells, and its sounds. Nothing else reaches in here, where the earth lies tiredly exposed, split open to the manic pummeling of man in his lust for riches. For centuries the earth has been ravaged, gnawed, and bitten, yet she lies there, uncaring, unresponsive. *How long?* Raimoti wonders. *How long will she take it before she decides it is enough? How long before she crushes the perpetrators in one gigantic twitch of her loins? How long before the Beast, nestling within her, emerges to swallow these plunderers? Not long,* the whispers echo behind him, pricking his scalp, making him break into a cold sweat. He turns around to find only the receding vision of the tunnel before it bends out of sight. The bats of fear fly twittering away from him into the crisscrossed web of abandoned gullies. They hear the Beast!

"What was that?" Raimoti screams, throwing down his shovel. His eyes wide open, his mouth dry, he listens intently for the footfall. *Thump!* It comes, only a wraith—unclear, unformed. *Haahaa-humph!* it chortles, a little louder.

"What is it, *kaka*?" Arif asks, putting down the pickax.

"I heard it! It's on the other side of that face!"

"What? Are you drunk, *kaka*? Or has coal filled your senile brain? What do you hear?"

"Hushsh! Listen."

The gang is shaken and they strive to listen. No one breathes. The only sound they hear is their own heartbeats, thumping nervously like a tambourine within their heaving chests. The stillness is absolute. The silence complete. After an interminable moment they hear a sound. Faint but true: *chchapp! gglugg!* Like a little bubble bursting to the surface. Then silence again. Nothing. They wait, but still there is nothing.

"*Chalo, bahin-chodon!* Work," Arif says finally. "It's nothing. This crazy old man will frighten us to death. It was probably his empty stomach revolting against all that *hadia* he had before coming down. Do us a favor, *kaka*. Go and crap somewhere so we don't have to suffer your bowel sounds again."

Raimoti stands still. He can't be mistaken. He has dreamed of it too often. His father and his grandfather described it too well. "At first it will sound like a massive bubble," they said. "Then there will be creaking, as of a cot under a fat woman. Then there will be rumbles, followed by a deafening crash. Then you will die."

There is a dry creak from behind the wall in front of the gang. Arif hesitates a moment, then shrugs. He lifts the pickax in his burnt-brown and sinewy arms and swings it down with all his might.

A small chunk of coal falls off, no bigger than a man's head. Then they notice the trickle. At first it is just a slick, quite common in the underground. But soon it grows into a thin jet of icy water—almost like the stream of urine Arif spouted.

It's the first claw of the Beast.

They hear an ominous rumble from within.

chapter 2

Water sloshes enticingly over huge cubes of ice in the whiskey glasses. Soda is scarce in this remote corner of the world. Bibhash Mukherjee offers the ambercool glasses to his guests. Winter has yet to set in, and a chilled drink at the end of a day is still refreshing in this parched land. Bibhash is in his forties and a mining engineer by qualification. He is a swarthy man of average build and sports a curly beard to underline his perpetually surly expression. He has soft, long fingers that are tipped with nicotine-stained and dirt-crusted nails. He has an obnoxious habit of digging out the dirt and rolling it into tiny pellets that he drops all around himself.

Born and brought up in Calcutta, he once used to have fine sensibilities and ambition. But endless years in this barren, subterranean job have blunted him. He hates being where he is and detests himself for it. He had a lucrative offer to join a large multinational company manufacturing mining equipment after graduating from the prestigious Institute of Mines, but he chose to pursue what he then felt was a "romantically adventurous profession" in a public sector company, despite the uninspiring salary. His disillusionment with his job has been fast and complete.

As the subarea manager for this godforsaken mine, he must spend most of his days in desolation, deep in the interior of nowhere. For days, sometimes weeks, he does not get a chance to visit his family in the city, only 180 kilometers away but a full nine hours of driving time on the pitiable roads of the gouged-out mining country. It is a hard life, and Bibhash is essentially a soft man.

His esteemed guests this evening are *Shri* Ram Krishna Pandey, general manager of personnel, and *Shri* Atul Karna, the mysterious visitor from that remote nebula simply called "the ministry" by executives and workers of the company. Karna *sahib* is so thin that he appears almost two-dimensional. His tight little beer belly is his only three-dimensional contour, betraying his fondness for drinking and the deskbound nature of his job. He is a slow talker, and his utterances are enveloped within prolonged pauses and hesitant mumbles. He is a fairy from the rarefied realms of power, completely out of depth and lost in these harsh surroundings. Though quite young, Karna *sahib* seems to wield considerable clout and influence.

The headquarters called up early that morning to prepare Bibhash for the visit. Karna *sahib* was sent by the ministry to study electronic data processing at the company and expressed his desire to visit an underground mine. Bibhash's subarea of the Kariakhani Mines was chosen precisely because there is so little work in progress here. The more you show, the liaison from headquarters explained conspiratorially, the more you expose, and that would be quite indecent, wouldn't it, now? So keep Karna *sahib* occupied and well entertained, the man enjoined.

Intricacies of hierarchies and chains of command in bureaucracy and state-owned enterprises are quite complex, and despite having spent many years in his job, Bibhash is still a little unclear about it. What he knows, though, is that the ultimate "ownership" of a public sector company is vested in the "people," but every simple worker understands this really means that some minister is the lord and master. In a democracy, the people's representative is more of a king than Caesar.

Bibhash knows only that in this democracy, ministers are ensconced within a cocoon of multilayered bureaucracy, with an elite bunch of federal civil servants at the top. Typically, they come from well-off urban families and top educational institutions. They are trained to believe that they are inherently superior to the technocrats and leave no opportunity to impress this fact upon whomever happens across their path. But not to be outdone, whenever they can, the technocrats use technicalities to obfuscate issues and neutralize the bureaucrats. It is a perpetual game of brinkmanship between the two. In the past, Bibhash has had a few bitter experiences with some overweening federal officers and has begun to understand why his parents always wanted him to become one of them rather than waste his life as a mining engineer. But at that time, he wasn't willing to go through the yearlong examination process and the even more grueling selection process for joining the civil services, where barely five hundred out of more than four hundred thousand applicants qualify annually.

In what is largely a centralized system of governance, these federal officers wield considerable power and influence on the professional management of state-owned enterprises.

Often a couple of bureaucrats are nominated to the board of directors of these companies. The board itself consists of the seniormost technocrats of the company—engineers and managers with a flair for politics and some ambition. Within the company, directors are like feudal lords, and some like to run the company as a personal fiefdom. Despite their unbridled powers in the company, quite frequently, they are maneuvered by the career bureaucrats in the ministry who have the "ears" of the political masters. So someone like Bibhash, who has almost a decade and a half of experience working in mines, is considered way below a much younger bureaucrat with just a few years of job experience.

Similarly, although mining is a very technical activity, the general managers and chief general managers of personnel are usually very influential people, due to the extreme volatility of mine workers and the impact of industrial relations on the company's financial health. By virtue of their job, managers of personnel are close to local political leaders and activists. They also have access to the directors, which is difficult for operations engineers located in remote mining areas. Even engineers who rise to the levels of general or chief general mangers of operations acquire a slightly political tint. But Bibhash is not likely to reach that rank in his career—or at best, he may reach it just before his retirement. He is not worldly enough. These things used to bother Bibhash in his early years. But now he takes them as postulates.

The importance of Karna *sahib* is underscored by the fact that a senior and high-profile general manager like Pandey*ji* has been asked to escort him. Mercifully, they will be leaving early next morning, as Karna *sahib* has to catch a train back in the afternoon. Mercifully, because as much as Bibhash misses company, he also hates visitors, who callously dive in to the narcotic tranquillity of his solitude only to fly off, leaving behind turbulent ripples of utter loneliness.

Ranjish hi sahi, dil hi dukhane ke liye aa. / *Aa fir se mujhe chchod ke jaane ke liye aa* . . . Wallowing in self-pity, he ruefully remembers the opening couplet from his favorite *ghazal*. Even if you have any grievances, just come to torment my heart. Come over, if only to abandon me again. As happens so often with him, his mind lapses into poetic reflections on borrowed words and thoughts. Lines from some favorite poet or even songs spring to his mind and hold silent conversations with him. He is Eleanor Rigby and Tithonus rolled into one, eternally lonely and yearning for redemption. Underground, he fancies being Lucifer: disgruntled, discarded, and disgraced by a heartless divinity. But for now he relishes each moment of this opportunity to share a drink and talk to people in English, even if he has to play the servile subordinate.

"It's a nice little guesthouse," Karna *sahib* remarks politely, sipping his drink.

"Thank you, *saar*! Heh heh." Pandey*ji* is alert to the tiniest worms of appreciation and laps them up with the dexterity of a lizard. He is a plump, pimply man in his early fifties and has crawled his way up the wall of success by preying on opportunities and spitting venom on competitors. He spares no effort to please anyone who is someone, and he ruthlessly tramples anybody who is nobody. He is insufferable and successful. Bibhash wishes to be as slimy and contented.

"Ah, the AC feels nice, doesn't it?" Karna *sahib* continues languorously.

"*Saar, saar,* absolutely, *saar.*" Pandey*ji* nods in agreement. "We've had the room chilled for you since morning, *saar.*"

As if he personally switched the damn thing on, Bibhash thinks glumly. They sit in silence for a while, Karna *sahib* with an inscrutable, faraway look in his flat eyes; Pandey*ji* looking adoringly at his guest; and Bibhash with a disconcertingly vacuous expression. He wears it often in company. He feels uncomfortable talking to strangers who may talk about unfamiliar things and expect an exchange of views. Bibhash stopped holding views on anything after realizing how often he was considered wrong and how inconsequential his opinions were to most people. He has long lost his ability to talk about anything that is not purely technical or related to work.

It's not that he is dumb or inarticulate. It's just that more often than not, he doesn't know what to say, and when he does know, he doesn't care enough to say anything. In his college days, he was considered a good elocutionist and was known for his sharp wit and tongue. But years of coal dust have made his mouth too dry. Mining is a tough profession, and mining engineers are not renowned for their sparkling wit or bonhomie. He has spent years in the company of people who are mechanical-minded and singularly unexciting. His witticisms and tongue-in-cheek remarks either have perplexed his colleagues and superiors or, worse, affronted them. Some thought he was crazy, while others suspected that he was smarter than he appeared and felt vaguely intimidated. In either case, Bibhash managed to lose friends faster than he gained years in experience. Gradually, he learned to appear as blunt as his colleagues wished him to be and, over time, has acquired a reticence that is frequently misinterpreted as obtuseness.

Having little ambition and even less perseverance, Bibhash has settled down in his role as a man who won't go anywhere in life. He has fallen out of the rat race where junior engineers try to outperform their peers in order to be counted on some list. From his initial status as a young executive with solid education and promise, he has slid below the line of vision of most chief managers. He is certain that no director even knows his name. They have no interest in his existence, and he reciprocates their feelings wholeheartedly.

At an intellectual level, he feels restless. So he has created a separate world for himself—of books, music, and generous doses of alcohol. Sometimes he feels that despite being from a higher social stratum, he is no better than the labor working under him. His distaste for the day ahead matches his disgust with the day gone by. Only drinking provides relief.

But his desires are not all dead, he realizes with regret as he sips his whiskey morosely. Buddha, he acknowledges, was correct: The world is full of suffering; desires are the root cause of suffering; to remove suffering, one must vanquish desires. He has tried, but he can't be the Buddha. He likes his whiskey a little too much for enlightenment. In fact, most of the time he is not sure if he has any real desires left or if he just suffers from a longing for desires.

He longs to be a good son, but his parents are many years

dead. He longs to be a loving husband, but his wife has drifted away. He longs to be a proud father, but his daughters are also distant. He longs to be a crisp professional, but he is too diffused. He longs for inner peace, but his thoughts twist like a tornado. He longs for soda in his drink, but there is none.

"Too bad there is no soda, though." The pompous bloody Karna *sahib* has to drive it home just then.

"So—sooo sorry, *saar. Arrey bhai*, Bibhash," says Pandey*ji*, immediately disassociating himself from the shortcoming. "Why didn't you get some soda from the city? If only you had told me, I would have arranged it. You have this tendency to overlook details. So sorry, *saar*, next time we will make proper arrangements."

Overtly, Bibhash continues his dull gaze and tries to look contrite, almost succeeding. Inside, he feels incinerated. He has met Pandey*ji* a few times before, and their dislike was instantaneous and mutual. Right now he feels like pouncing on Pandey and throttling the fat pig till he squeals and turns blue. But he just doesn't have it in him. "So sorry, sir" is all Bibhash can say.

"Never mind, never mind," Karna *sahib* drawls generously, absently putting a piece of overcooked *tikka* in his mouth. "I was only mentioning it. Umm—nice *tikkas*!"

"I cooked it," Bibhash lies shamelessly, wanting to see Pandey*ji*'s reaction. He is delighted to observe the scowl on his senior's face.

"Oh, incidentally, *saar*," Pandey*ji* says, quickly changing the topic, "how was your trip underground? I hope you enjoyed yourself, *saar*. It is usually a great experience for any outsider. So sorry I was tied up with some other work."

Pandey*ji* had actually retired for a quick nap, leaving Bibhash to attend to the unsavory task of showing Karna *sahib* around the mines.

"I'm sure, I'm sure," Karna *sahib* replies edgily. "But unfortunately, I couldn't go down. You see, I am—um—allergic to dust, and once I reached the pit, my sinuses started acting up. Didn't want to risk being taken ill, you know? Have this damn meeting with the minister to attend as soon as I reach back. But yes, I had—er—a little peek inside the shaft, and boy, was it dark! Hope you people can see what you are doing down there—ha!"

"We usually want to avoid doing that, sir," Bibhash says blandly, draining his glass. "We are there to turn a blind eye, if you know what I mean, sir."

"Ha-ha!" Pandey*ji* coughs nervously, staring angrily at his subordinate. Now he realizes why Bibhash has been posted to this wretched place. "Bibhash has a great sense of humor, *saar*. Actually, *saar*, the underground is well lit nowadays, and besides, we wear torches on our helmets."

"The better to see you with!" Karna *sahib* quips with a dry laugh. Bibhash, an alumnus of the prestigious La Marts school in Calcutta, joins him. Pandey*ji* looks puzzled but laughs nevertheless.

"So, tell me," Karna *sahib* continues after a long pause, "how do you go about—ah—digging these damn dungeons?"

Pandey*ji,* more of a manager than a miner, looks at Bibhash for a reply. Bibhash fights a strong urge to tell Karna *sahib* that he wouldn't understand. At the same time, he feels a servile need to please the bureaucrat. He is fed up with his wretched and lonesome existence in Kariakhani and wants out. He wants to give life one more try. He thinks he will be a little less unsuccessful as a staff officer in the corporate headquarters. He was born and brought up in urban surroundings and is completely out of place in this wilderness. He wants to reconnect with his wife and children or at least make a sincere last attempt before giving up.

It is very rare that he gets to meet anyone from the ministry, and Karna may hold a key to his redemption—maybe Bibhash can create an opening to request Karna *sahib*'s intervention for seeking a transfer to the company headquarters. More than anything, he wants to put Pandey in his place. Granted, the man is a general manager of personnel, but he has to be made to understand that Bibhash is the engineer in charge of this mine and knows more about it. As a subarea manager, Bibhash is responsible for practically every aspect of the mine, the equipment, safety, and welfare of the men working there. This is his one chance to impress someone important with his technical knowledge and expertise. It's not going to be easy for Bibhash, unaccustomed as he is to the nuances of lobbying. But desperation drives him to make an attempt. If Karna *sahib* can be impressed, Bibhash can make a direct request before the man leaves in the morning. Even directors will listen to someone like Karna *sahib*. So Bibhash decides to lay it on thick and sound like the hard-core professional that he isn't. Surely the bureaucrat will see how someone as brilliant as Bibhash is needed in the headquarters rather than wasting himself in a dying mine like Kariakhani.

"Well, to start at the beginning," Bibhash says, refilling all the glasses, "we first do a geological survey of the coal-bearing area and determine the amount and expanse of the coal bed. If the overburden—the layer of earth above the coal seam—is thin, we opt for what is called an open-cast mine. If, on the other hand, the crust is too thick, we drill to allow for underground mining. There are two main techniques of underground mining: the board-and-pillar method and the longwall. Here, we use the former method."

Bibhash stops to ascertain if he has grabbed Karna *sahib*'s attention. He finds Karna gazing attentively at a moth sitting motionlessly on the opposite wall. This, Bibhash thinks bravely, could mean that the man is hooked. Or, he worries miserably, that Karna has switched off completely.

Bibhash takes a huge, nervous gulp of the whiskey and casts a sideways glance at Pandey*ji*, who reclines in an armchair with the impassivity of a water buffalo chewing the cud. He is watching Bibhash carefully, trying to figure out if he needs to intervene. He doesn't want the silly fellow to make any loose talk that may embarrass the bosses. But so far, Bibhash has caused no damage. Rather, by veering into absurd technical details, he will provide Karna *sahib* with authentic local flavor that will enhance his mine-visit experience. Or so Pandey*ji* thinks.

Finding neither encouragement nor discouragement, Bibhash gets a little unsure of himself and loses steam. He looks at Pandey*ji* again for a sign. Pandey judges that Karna has no objection and gives Bibhash a brief nod, digging the cracks of his teeth with a toothpick to dislodge some bits of the *tikkas* he has just devoured.

"Put simply," Bibhash resumes, clearing his throat, "we drill a tunnel or well, called an incline or shaft, down to the coal bed and then dig horizontally through the seam, creating a network of

galleries. We leave massive columns—pillars of coal at the inter-
sections—as supports, and make tunnels, extracting the mineral
as we progress. Strange as it may sound, this is called the development phase. The greater the development, the more hollow it
grows. Something like the state of the nation, one might say, sir—
ha, ha!"

He is relieved to find a slow smile playing on Karna's lips,
while Pandey's beady eyes narrow with suspicion. Civil servants
like to think they run the country, he reflects, and one should take
care when commenting on issues like the state of the nation. But
happily, Karna *sahib* has found something worth smiling at in Bibhash's words, so there is no need to worry.

"Anyway, once we have reached as far as possible, we retreat, depillaring the columns of coal behind us. That is called
the extraction phase," Bibhash says, noting the empty glass in
Karna's hands. He quickly finishes off his own and pours a drink
for Karna. Pandey*ji* also extends his glass for a refill. Reluctantly,
Bibhash fills it up.

"Most of the eight mines here are in the development phase,"
Bibhash continues, feeling a little light-headed and riding on a
new confidence generated by Karna's smile, "except Mines Number One and Two, where we have almost completed extraction.
Mine Number Three, which is the closest, is in the final phase of
development."

"Hmm—sounds intriguing. Can I get some more ice,
please?"

Karna *sahib* looks far from intrigued as he taps his foot gently
in time with the *ghazal* playing softly in the background. He feels

obliged to ask some more questions just to keep the conversation going. It has been the same story with everyone he has met on this trip, he feels. They can only talk abstruse gibberish about the damn mines and the coal. They are like human moles in their thinking and conduct, suffering from tunnel vision and totally lacking perspective. But he sighs softly: One must communicate with these creatures and learn something. It might come in handy back in the ministry to impress bosses. Besides, he has this streak of Desmond Morris in him and enjoys studying diverse specimens of humanity.

"Must be a bit tough on the buggers who dig down there," Karna *sahib* comments compassionately, popping a couple of hot *pakoras* into his thin mouth.

"Not as tough as you suspect, *saar*," Pandey*ji* says soothingly. "We take good care of our employees. But the bastards are never happy. We have given them houses, schools, and hospitals. We pay them well, and yet they are constantly complaining about the conditions of work. Hah! They should have worked in those private mines before nationalization, or they could try the privately held rat holes of the northeast. These human rights activists and the local leaders, *neta-log*, have really spoiled the sons of bitches. Can't afford to pamper them too much, *saar*."

"Umm—certainly, certainly," Karna *sahib* agrees. "You can't succumb to blackmailing by labor unions. But surely, some— ah—demands must be genuine? How unsafe is it in the undergrounds?"

"Oh! It is quite safe now, as Bibhash will explain to you, *saar*. Bibhash?"

"Well, sir," Bibhash replies uncomfortably, not knowing the extent of truthfulness expected of him, "the conditions are definitely much better, but the risk involved is undeniable. Despite the stringent safety norms and regular inspections, the probability of accidents resulting in injury or even death is fairly high. Risk is implicit in this business. As they say of all the peacetime professions, mining is the most hazardous."

"Oh! Yes. I've heard that quoted quite regularly by you chaps. But why don't you people do something about it? I mean, why should the government act as a nanny to the industry?"

"It doesn't, sir," Bibhash retorts, prying some dirt from under his nails. "Pardon my saying so, but we feel that the government is far removed from the ground—or should I say underground—realities. Also, the newfound commercial zest of the government forces the management to take risks."

"You think so?" Karna *sahib* asks, looking surprised. "What does profit orientation have to do with safety?"

Bibhash is annoyed by Karna *sahib*'s supercilious breeziness. He knows that only unfortunate circumstances have placed him in an inferior position to the holiday-minded Karna and the pompously plebeian Pandey*ji*. He finds the temptation to exploit this opportunity to smother an officer from the ministry with technicalities peevishly irresistible; also, he has a cloying urge to remind Pandey*ji* of his redundancy in the grim surroundings of a working coal mine. At school, he was considered an excellent orator.

"Sir," Bibhash replies ponderously, deliberately fixing his gaze on Pandey*ji*, "public sector companies are managed by technocrats who want good appraisals for their promotions. The main requirement for that today is increased production. So there is an element of ruthlessness involved. The pressure to increase production is constantly mounting, and managers pass it down the line. Unfortunately, the breaking point occurs in the mines where few senior executives venture regularly. It is the lowliest of workers who pays for it. We push our limited capabilities in terms of technology and expertise to the extreme, leaving little margin for errors. The result at times is disastrous."

Karna looks perturbed. He isn't sure if he quite likes the imputation the subarea manager seems to be making about governance. What does the bugger know about running a country or policy making? He frowns, making Pandey squirm in his chair. "I hope you realize that the company or its managers don't function independently of the government's policies. Perhaps you public sector chaps resent the fact that the ministry insists upon performance and delivery," Karna says sternly, wiping his hands delicately with a linen napkin.

"Of course, *saar*. Of course, *saar*," Pandey*ji* whines ingratiatingly. "We—the board is completely guided by the policies and intent of the ministry."

"I don't see how you can say that our policies are responsible for endangering workers," Karna persists peevishly. "We in the ministry are far more aware and concerned about the condition of workers—at a macro level, they are human resources, not labor. I don't know what exactly you mean."

"Let me explain through an example," Bibhash continues, ignoring desperate glances and signals from Pandey. "We have Mine Number Three close by, which, as I said, is in the final phases of development. Currently, we have about fifty workers per shift mining out the last possible kilo of coal from the seam. The seam was quite thick, about twenty meters. But the overburden, the soil above the deposit of coal, was more than eighty meters. So we went for the underground method. Over the last decade or so, we have reached the boundaries of the coal bed. On one side, we have a lake, which has recently been flooded. We are now working within a hundred meters of the last mapped margin of water, barely outside the sixty-meter limit prescribed by the director general of mine safety. Mostly, we use small-explosive charges to dislodge coal, and these can be a bit unreliable at times. In places, the corridors are so narrow and close to underground extensions of the lake that we have even resorted to the archaic method of manual cutting."

"What's that?" Karna *sahib* quizzes, regaining composure. He can't let a mere mining engineer rile him. The poor fellow is probably tipsy. He decides to humor Bibhash and hear out his gibberish. "Sounds like a term more suited for a tailoring shop," he remarks, sipping from his glass.

"Historically, cutters were specialized workers who used pick-axes to dig coal," Bibhash continues more soberly. He has realized that he came too close to crossing the line that separates the fairies from the ghouls. He tries to sound dispassionately academic to soothe ruffled feathers. "The practice has largely been discontinued in the last couple of decades. But in rare instances, we still use this method, primarily to maximize production. Now, in Mine Number Three, we also use the weakest, the most troublesome, and the least desirable of our workmen. It is a form of punishment. Production by manual cutting is so low that the market value of coal extracted by one worker per shift is lower than his wages. It is not easy to sack a worker nowadays; hence, it is better to keep these workers occupied—at least they are down under, digging away and not causing trouble. So instead of using explosives, we use cutters who can go in closer to the water without puncturing the walls. We get some more tons to add to our target and solve a potential labor problem. Lately, there have been some reports of seepage, but we've had it inspected, and our surveyors have found the locations where work is in progress to be quite safe. There is a slight risk—there always is—but I have been directed to continue in the overall interest of this area. That is what I meant when I said we are supposed to turn a blind eye to things."

"But surely there is some way to remove such workers who have become—umm—unproductive? What about dismissal, hmm? After all, you do discard dilapidated and worn-out machines, don't you?" Karna *sahib* inquires distractedly, fast losing interest. He has had enough of coal talk for the night. He wishes the damn fellow would turn off.

But Bibhash doesn't know when to let it be. That's the secret of his unpopularity. "Machines don't form unions, sir, and they don't cast votes." Bibhash persists on his theme, impervious to Pandey's murderous glares. "Dismissal always involves drawn-out procedures and often ends up in litigation. We do have a scheme for voluntary retirement, which we use to encourage the unwanted laborers to leave. In this Mine Number Three itself, we have a rather well-known worker, Raimoti, who is quite old. In fact, we suspect that his age records have been doctored, but we have no proof. He is also addicted to *hadia* and ganja. But since he is quite popular among the workers, any attempt to dismiss him will give the unions an excuse to trouble us. He is approaching the age for voluntary retirement, and we have made it clear to him that we don't expect him to continue beyond that. It is simpler that way."

"Ah—yes indeed. Talented cook you've got here!" Karna *sahib* compliments no one in particular. *If the man won't stop,* Karna thinks, *he should be tactfully snubbed.* Pandeyji grins conspiratorially, dumping a large helping of the snacks on Karna *sahib*'s greasy plate.

It is getting late, and Pandey*ji* tells an attendant lurking in the background to get the dinner laid. Moving to a rudimentary dining room, they sit down to an elaborate feast prepared by the guesthouse cook in honor of the important personage. The hall is not air-conditioned, so they sit sweating malodorously in the whiskey-enhanced heat and talk desultorily about the process of mining and the difficulties of managing a bunch of uncouth, undisciplined, and ungrateful workmen. Karna has surrendered himself to the topic. Try as he might, he can't get them to talk about anything else. Pandey*ji* is at his lyrical best as he praises his own contribution to the area. Bibhash is disgusted but nods enthusiastically in agreement. An offended personnel manager can ensure that he grows old in Kariakhani.

Suddenly, they hear a commotion outside, and a few harried-looking men in mining gear rush in. The men scream and shout, babbling incoherently till Pandey*ji* lets loose a fulsome stream of expletives and asks them to shut up. Then he turns to a man and says, "*Ai!* Ram Babu, what happened? *Arre saala,* can't you see we are having dinner?"

"*M-maafi, s-sahib,*" the panic-stricken foreman replies between deep gasps of breath, "but Mine Number Three is flooding. Most of the gangs working underground have managed to evacuate, but about ten or fifteen miners are yet to come out. We have sent four rescue workers down to assess the situation, but it appears quite serious, *sahib*. We can hear the sound of water at the mouth of the shaft. It sounds like a river run wild!"

chapter 3

Madho winces at the shrill voice of his wife synthesizing appropriately and sibilantly with the hiss and splatter of water spraying from the fancy faucet of their newly installed shower. Dolly is a terrible singer, but he dare not say so. She has been in the shower over a quarter of an hour, screeching out one tuneless ditty after another.

"Hui! Hui! Hui!" comes the scream. *"Main mast! Han-han mast!* I am turned on," sings Dolly, "yes, I am." It's a rather old movie number, but one that Dolly likes.

Madho wishes Dolly could sing as well as she fucks. Just the thought of her creamy, plump breasts and buttocks jiggling under the shower makes him squirm with anticipated ecstasy. Tomorrow is his day off, and as is their ritual, they will eat and drink in front of their fourteen-inch color TV till the children fall asleep, and then they will copulate violently to sleep. Almost three years of marriage have not dampened Madho's ardor and pitiable passion for Dolly.

In the bathroom, Dolly finishes her shower and stands for a while, relishing the cool, wet feeling. All over. She looks down and pouts unhappily at her slightly sagging breasts and bulging belly. She stands straight and tries to peer down at her toes without bending her neck. Someone has told her that if you can't see your toes that way, it means you have a paunch. She is dismayed to find that she can't. She bends her head a little and then a little more till she finally spots her toes and smiles. She has been on a fruit diet for two weeks, and today she feels that she has to crane her neck a bit less to view her toes. She must be slimming down! She then grabs her love handles and is satisfied; they feel less spongy.

Dolly steps out of the shower stall and grabs the towel from a hook behind the plywood door. She dries herself energetically and stands next to the half-length mirror she insisted on having installed in the tiny bathroom. She ties the towel on her head like a turban to soak up the excess water, and she notes that her armpits need another shave. Since she is one of the few women in the settlement who dare to wear sleeveless blouses, she has to be careful.

She remembers her hometown in that lovely port town in the Deep South. Since theirs is a matriarchal society, women there are far more liberated, and even her mother used to wear skirts and sleeveless tops. Of course, Dolly has only a faint memory of her mother, who died of some unmentionable disease when Dolly was eleven. She used to run a small lodge for sailors and made delicious *appams* and fish in coconut gravy. On Sundays and holidays, she spent hours oiling and combing Dolly's hair with coconut oil as she sang softly under her breath. That is where Dolly inherited her vocal talents. She vaguely remembers being happy and contented in her childhood.

She doesn't remember her father at all. He was a sous chef on a passenger liner between her hometown and the Middle East. But after Dolly's birth, the frequency of his visits to his home port reduced to fewer than once a year. Whenever he came, he brought foreign toys, clothes, shoes, and trinkets for his daughter. The last time Dolly saw him was a few months after her mother's death, when he left with promises to take her away after a couple of years. But that never happened.

Dolly was brought up by her grandmother, a venerable and enterprising woman with a deep hatred for men that could come only from excessive love gone unrequited. A year after the death of Dolly's mother, she made a deal with a local doctor to open a polyclinic in the lodge. Dr. Menon had recently left a state hospital and wanted to start his own nursing home, which he called Angels' Clinic. The old woman ensured that Dolly got an education and enrolled her in a nursing course at sixteen. She firmly believed that a young woman should be financially self-reliant.

She also instilled in her granddaughter a sense of independence and competence and taught her that surviving in a man's world required a girl to learn some guiles. Dolly's grandmother took her to the locally famous Paris Parlor hair salon, where her luscious long hair was butchered into a trendy bobbed cut. At first Dolly was resentful of losing the tresses her mother had nurtured with so much love and oil, but she quickly changed her mind when street Romeos started whistling at her as she walked down to her nursing classes. When she told her granny about it, the old woman just smiled and said, "Power doesn't only mean muscles."

Now Dolly bends down to review the condiments of femininity stacked on a small plastic table below the mirror, and picks out a face cream. When she looks at herself in the mirror, a young woman who should be looking younger stares back at her. Women shouldn't age, she concludes with a sigh. It makes them ugly. Then she perks up a bit, reasoning that she isn't old. No longer in her first bloom but definitely not old. She resents that men don't have to worry that much about age.

She remembers herself as a young woman, full of life and optimism: fresh, eager, confident, and sporting bobbed hair. When, at eighteen, she lost her virginity in a few exploratory seconds to a neighbor's teenage son, she concluded that sex was overrated. But on a drenched monsoon afternoon when she was seduced by the prosperous middle-aged doctor who ran the polyclinic, she realized that sex was also *power*. The doctor had a paralytic wife whom he worshipped, and therefore he fucked Dolly several times with a religious fervor. When he ejaculated, he called out his wife's name in ecstasy—or remorse, Dolly couldn't be certain. That rainy afternoon she crossed over from girlhood to womanhood and wept under the burden. The satiated and grateful doctor misunderstood it and forced an irresistible amount of cash on her when she left his examination room. His valedictory kisses accompanied petitions for future trysts and promises of more cash. He was a good man. She had her third realization of the day: that tears also have power over men. With three realizations in just one day, some men have attained enlightenment.

When she returned home, her granny met her at the door and took in her flushed and disheveled appearance without a word. Granny's eyes flashed a strobe of questions from behind her thick glasses, forcing Dolly to lower her own to protect her thoughts from shriveling. Finally, her grandmother hugged her with the defeated smile of relief that only survivors possess.

Dolly applies her face cream with care and slowness that is almost sensuous. She likes touch, even of her own hands. She picks up a stick of kohl and, with deft fingers, blackens the rims of her lustrous eyes. She loves her eyes. They are dark brown and big enough to hold a hundred expressions at a time. They keep men guessing.

Throughout her course in nursing, she had an array of men who wanted to quiz her eyes and explore her body. She realized early that she didn't really mind that. Growing up with only her ma and then her grandmother, she always wondered what a man's touch would be like. As a child, when she watched other children in the neighborhood with their fathers or brothers, she wanted to experience a man's touch. Initially, it came as a surprise to her that men wanted to touch her very differently from what she had imagined as a child. But she liked it nevertheless. That men felt obliged to compensate her in some way for being allowed to do so was an unexpected gain for Dolly. She never felt wrong letting them. Maybe she was different from other girls her age. But she had a different history, she guessed.

After completing her diploma in nursing, she joined the Angels' Clinic for about a year. The pay was good, and Dr. Menon was very accommodating. Although his ardor had diminished, Dolly could always be certain to find a place on his examination table whenever she needed some extra money. He could never say no to her, though she got a feeling that he wanted to. After conquests, men turn into cowards.

That winter another doctor who worked for some public sector coal company was admitted to the Angels' Clinic. He was on a vacation to the South with his family and had the misfortune of contracting typhoid. His condition was so bad that the polyclinic doctors prohibited travel and advised immediate hospitalization. He spent six weeks in Dolly's care. After the initial week, his wife and two children returned because it was too expensive for them to continue staying in a hotel. The doctor assured his family that he was in good hands and would follow as soon as he was strong enough to travel.

Since winter is a "bad" month for clinics—not too many people fall ill with malaria or cholera—the Angels' Clinic was nearly empty. Dolly and the three other nurses of the ten-bed facility didn't have too much work. Dr. Sen occupied the only single-bed intensive-care room of the nursing home, which had a large window that overlooked the rocky beach across the road. It entitled him to a twenty-four-hour dedicated nurse. Being the most junior, Dolly was assigned the evening-to-morning shift. She didn't mind it much, since during the first fortnight, the patient slept through most of her shift, requiring nothing more of her than taking his temperature every few hours and giving him his medicines. Dolly spent the time reading fashion magazines or secondhand Mills & Boon romances.

Sen, a mild-mannered man of about thirty with clean, pleasant features, was the ideal patient. Once his condition improved, he gave Dolly money to buy him some books to read. He also asked her to get him a sketchbook and some charcoal pencils. When Dolly came in around six in the evening, she would find him quietly reading or sketching. Gradually, they started chatting. He was very different from the men Dolly had met up till then. He was supremely intelligent, well read, and sensitive, with a slightly forlorn attitude that Dolly was later to identify with the depressing surroundings of coalfields. He was curious about her childhood, commiserated with the loss of her mother, and expressed anger about her father's abandonment. He was a good artist and one day surprised Dolly with his evocative pencil sketches of her. He had sketched her as she read or gazed out the window. She liked the play of light and shade that he managed with a few strokes. For the first time, she felt special. For the first time, she found herself a little breathless when she sponged him in the mornings before ending her shift. She liked the suppleness of his body and his smell.

One night, as she dozed in her armchair, she sensed someone close to her. With a start, she opened her eyes and turned on the bedside lamp. She found Dr. Sen standing over her, looking startled in the dim light. Worried that he was feeling unwell, she tried to get up. But her patient pushed her back in the chair and just stayed there, looking longingly into her eyes but saying nothing. He looked vulnerable and miserable in the guiltyellow light. Dolly felt a sudden surge of love and a deep sense of compassion and quietly turned off the light. Then they did what men and women do best together when lonely.

Dolly knew love for the first time in her young life. The next few weeks passed in a rosy daze for her. Sen was improving fast, and sometimes they would go for short strolls along the seaside. To the world, they were a patient and a caring nurse. But there was a far heavier emotion that Dolly carried in her heart when she walked with Dr. Sen. He told her about his childhood and narrated hilarious tales of his medical-school days. He told her about his mother and aunts and discussed the insipidity of his wife and the ennui of his married life. No other man had invited Dolly so deep into his heart, and she was thrilled.

He was her doorway to another life and a new world. Every day he discovered something new to praise in her. Every night he showed her a new method of exchanging love. Sometimes they pretended they were married with many kids and even enacted occasional fights over imaginary household matters. In that sleepy, inconsequential town, no one suspected that two people had conjured a beautiful and private world that was totally invisible to anyone else. At nineteen, Dolly was a believer in possibilities and could not see the harsh boundaries that divided reality from dreams.

At the end of six weeks, Dr. Menon declared Sen completely cured of typhoid. Sen went home the next day, leaving behind a sheaf of charcoal sketches of Dolly and a promise to get her a job in his company. Sen was an emotional man, and he wept as he boarded his train at the railway station, telling Dolly that he didn't know how he would survive without her. Dolly believed in his unspoken promises about a future together.

He was true to his word, and after a couple of months, Dolly received a letter enclosing an application form for a nursing job in the medical services of the coal company Sen worked for. Like all good men, he fulfilled his obligations. She did not worry too much that the letter was formal and distant. *Men can get so tongue-tied in love,* she thought with a smile. It was obvious how much Sen wanted her with him.

Dolly was ecstatic and sent off the application. She got a call for an interview after a few weeks. When she told her grandmother about it, the old woman looked sad. But an opportunity to work in a state-owned hospital could not be ignored. Dolly would be settled for life.

It was going to be a long journey through four provinces, and her granny bought Dolly a ticket for an air-conditioned sleeper coach. On the night before her departure, Dolly's granny gave her a paper-wrapped package. Inside, she found a gold chain and a vanity box full of imported cosmetics available in stores for cheap smuggled goods supplied by merchant-navy sailors.

Now Dolly mulls for a while before choosing a brick-red glossy lipstick that enhances the juiciness of her lips. Her upper lip may be a bit thin, but the lower one curls out invitingly, igniting souls. She loves her lips as much as if not more than her eyes. And the shallow dimple on her left cheek.

Dr. Sen used to adore her dimple. He had come to receive her at the ramshackle station of a coal-mining town. The yard was crowded with wagons laden with black diamond from the neighboring coal mines, and the platforms were carpeted with coal dust. Sen had lightly brushed a hot hand across her cheek and felt her dimple with a trembling finger. They spent the night in a rundown hotel where Dolly learned that love hurts.

After four hours of cosmic lovemaking, Sen told her that he had ensured she would get the job, but he had been transferred to another company in the north, several hundred kilometers away. His family had already left, and he was taking a train the next morning. He had arranged and paid for a taxi that would take Dolly to the mining town where the company hospital was situated. He also pressed upon her five thousand rupees, saying that she would need it before she got her first salary. He said that he was sorry it had to be so but he had responsibilities that a man would not shirk. He was happy that Dolly had been a realistic woman from the start and understood these things. He knew that she would be all right and would have a great future in her new employment. He also assured that, whenever possible, he would visit her.

Dolly went numb and mutely accepted what was offered. As her heart froze, she opened her legs one last time to Dr. Sen. Early the next morning, Sen kissed her goodbye and left. Shortly after breakfast, the taxi he hired took Dolly to the hospital. She got the job and started a new life with no baggage. Her affair with Sen inoculated her against sentimentalism and romance.

A month later, when she found out she was pregnant, she decided to keep the child. The embryo was proof that once she had loved. She wrote to her granny, who came over with a false marriage certificate that convinced the company management Dolly had been married to a sailor who left her with a baby in her belly. Not many women would have made that tough call, but Dolly had been hardened by experience. She wrote to the good doctor, who replied promptly but never came. Instead, he sent her a generous money order that Dolly accepted dispassionately. It would not be easy bringing up a child as a single mother in that place. She would need his money and more still, and she had a fair idea how to get it.

There were many lonely men in the valleys of coal.

Her granny was a great help and support through her son's youth. He was the first male they could mold and pamper who loved them unconditionally. The two women doted on him. Dolly was thankful to have her granny living with them through those years. When the old lady died, her great-grandson was already ten and going to school. She had done her bit. Dolly was devastated for weeks but finally came out of it. She had learned young in life to put her own peace of mind before all else; she had learned that it was better to use others than to be used. So when she felt the need for a man to walk her through to old age, she decided to look for a husband who wouldn't run off.

Madho, the youngest and only surviving of Raimoti's siblings, is a passionate and ambitious man full of greed and vigor. He is gleaming black and muscular, even at forty-two. His hair has grayed prematurely, and he walks with a slight stoop acquired from years of working underground. He has puffy cheeks and hungryellow eyes that glow like embers in a heap of ash. Raimoti cared for him well after the death of their parents, and Madho passed his intermediate exam at the close of his schooling with good marks. He has slowly climbed up the promotion ladder to the E2 grade of a junior executive, and he hopes to rise further. Dolly wants him to.

He met Dolly a few years back in a company-owned medi-

cal clinic where she worked as a nurse. Madho had been admitted
there for three weeks with multiple fractures to his ribs—the result of a drunken fall down a tower-mounted Koepe winder that
he was repairing. One night, after helping Madho use the urinal,
Dolly noticed his enormous erection. Out of the sheer boredom
of an uneventful night shift and idle curiosity, she masturbated his
gigantic member in the darkness. She acquired yet another addict
to her acts of nursely compassion and repeated the ministration
several times before Madho was reluctantly discharged.

From these unexpected services rendered to immobilized patients, Dolly made a tidy supplement to her meager salary. Hardly
anyone protested. It was an easy and profitable avocation. The
fistful of depressed resident doctors serving time in that remote
health center was more demanding, but they also paid well. The
extra money came in handy for the upbringing of her only child,
Tommy, a bastard and a wastrel. She was a little over thirty when
she met Madho and realized that her charms, and therefore her sup-
plementary income, would not last. After a year or so of miserable
persuasion, she agreed to Madho's proposal for marriage, and she
had no regrets. Madho was energetic, had good prospects, and was
doglike in his devotion to her. The two teenage daughters from his
previous marriage were merely a temporary inconvenience. Now,
approaching forty, Dolly is glad she made the decision to marry
when she did. She has had a difficult life and feels entitled to some
comforts and stability. Life has taught her the art of manipulat-
ing, and she has no qualms about putting that to good use. Some
people consider her domineering, self-centered, or even crass, but
she doesn't care.

Madho's older daughter, Mona, is a spoiled, petulant girl of
sixteen, and Tina is three years younger. A brutal cesarean section for the delivery of Tina ruptured the uterus of their mother,
Lachchami, and rendered her incapable of bearing another child.
When Madho realized this, he tried to successively burn, drown,
and poison his wife, but he failed at every attempt. He finally became reconciled to a sonless existence and the apparent immortal-
ity of his ugly wife, until, eight years ago, in an act of divine jest,
Lachchami accidentally fell into the chemical pit of a washery and
was drowned, burned, and poisoned to death in the acid. Being
the elder, Mona is always pampered by Madho, while Tina is the
harbinger of sorrows and death. Now, on the threshold of womanhood, Mona has found a dubious role model in her stepmother,
Dolly. Mona dropped out of school after her tenth and spends all
her time dressing up, visiting friends, and watching soaps on TV.
She has many admirers in the colony of miners and is rather free
with her attention. She hopes to ensnare some suitable boy, prefer-
ably an executive, and marry as early as she can. Mona's premature
curves and cleavage have convinced Dolly that Mona will soon be
married and out of her hair. In fact, Dolly has been tutoring Mona
in the more active techniques of allurement, and Mona is a fine
pupil.

In contrast, Tina is short, frail, and ugly, a lot like her mother,
Lachchami. She has a forlorn look and a permanently unkempt
appearance. She is an exceptionally bright child and has been
awarded a scholarship from the company. She keeps to herself and
is the only one in the house who is close to Raimoti. Tina—like
her uncle and unlike her stepmother—is a natural singer. Some-

times, when Raimoti is in the mood, he lets her play the harmonium and sing along with him. He tells her that one day a prince will trap her in a golden cage and spirit her away, and she will sing like the cuckoo, happily ever after. She knows it will never happen. But her uncle always tries to encourage her talent. Just this afternoon, before going underground, Raimoti promised to give her a hundred rupees to buy a cassette of the latest filmy hits. She can then spend afternoons perfecting her favorite songs on Raimoti's battered old harmonium—she is the only one allowed to touch that mausoleum of Raimoti's dreams.

Dolly emerges, wet and voluptuous in her kaftan, humming a raunchy number under her breath and brushing her sparse shoulder-length hair. She finds Madho in front of the TV, sipping his rum, waiting with an empty glass for her. As she ambles to the little dresser in the corner, he reaches out and makes a grab at her, which she skillfully evades with a laugh. Madho always has sex on his mind on nights before his day off. Perhaps she should deny him the pleasure for a while, till he concedes to her demand to separate from Raimoti. Dolly finds Raimoti intolerable, with his hallucinatory vision of the world, his obsession with the Beast, and his sepulchral presence. Many a time she has tried to convince Madho to kick his zombie brother out but has failed. Madho maintains that he is indebted to Raimoti for his education. Besides, he says, Raimoti's contribution of half his salary is essential for their lavish living. Rubbish! Dolly feels. She can make up the loss with an increase in her night shifts at the clinic. She intends to have another go at Madho this evening.

"Come on, Dolly*ji*!" Madho pleads with his wife. "No need

to wear all that makeup. You look gorgeous as you are—in fact, the less you wear, the better you look."

"*Hatt! Besharam,*" Dolly croons back. "You can only think of all that. For you I am just a seminal spittoon, that's all. That's why you never listen to me."

"*Arre!* So come and sit by my side, and I will listen to your beautiful voice," Madho lies lasciviously.

Dolly comes to where Madho is sitting, and he pours out a drink for her. They watch the popular multimillion game show for some time, entranced by the steady flow of cash and goodies. One of the contestants walks away with a motorcycle, and the presenter announces a break.

Dolly sighs, taking a long swig. "Tommy would love a bike like that."

"Your son will be lucky if he ever acquires a cycle," Madho comments bravely. "All he does is run after girls and get into fights. If he doesn't pass his inter this time, no one will give him a job. He will remain a parasite on us all his life."

"Parasite? *Saala kamina!*" Dolly is instantly aflame, her luscious lips quivering with maternal indignation. "And what about your crazy brother? Is he not a parasite? And your filthy daughters? What are *they*? Goddess Laxami? *Arre!* If you want to set people right, first set your own life in order. I am sick of being the maid and provider for your clan. Ha! Tommy a parasite. *Arre, kuttey,* don't I bring home money? It is more than enough for my son and me. Had it not been for my love for you, I would have run away from this wretched house long ago. And look how you treat me—ooo-hooo!"

Dolly is a master in the art of bursting into tears. The kohl smudges and runs down her chubby cheeks in greasy, wet gray streaks of theatrical sorrow. Her button nose turns red with the effort, and she downs her glass in one angry swallow. Madho had not bargained for this outburst. Normally, he is quite circumspect about saying anything that might offend Dolly, but on rare occasions, his machismo overpowers his discretion, and the outcome is inevitably wet and wild. When will he learn?

"Enough, *enough*, Dolly*ji*," he pleads miserably. "Don't do that—here, take this towel—good, now take this drink—is it chilled? No no, don't smash it—yes, relax—calm down. Yes, now we will talk. Sorry—I *said* I'm sorry. I can't see you cry, Dolly*ji*— you *know* that!"

Dolly knows it very well, and once she is certain she has Madho's undivided attention, she switches off her tear ducts and turns on the heat. "Why don't you get a job for Tommy?" she asks querulously. "You don't do anything for him, while I slog my arse out for your daughters and your loony brother."

"I am trying, *baba*, I'm trying," Madho says patiently. "But since he has so little qualification, it is difficult. Still, I spoke to Mukherjee *sahib* and Tripurari *babu* to take him on as a *badli* worker. They have promised to do something soon."

"Huh! A *badli*!" Dolly snorts exquisitely. "What's so great about that? Anyone can become a temporary laborer in a mine."

"That's what you think!" Madho retorts irately. "Gone are those days when the mining *sirdars* came begging you to fill up a gap in the labor line. Today, even to join as a *badli* worker, you need the backing of an MP. I said I am trying, and as soon as there is a vacancy, I will meet Tripurari *babu* and ask him to put in a word with the MP *sahib*."

"I will be watching," Dolly says, a little mollified. "And what about your brother?"

"What about him? What has the poor fellow done now? He lives quietly in his unreal world, comfortably numb, under the haze of ganja and *hadia*—what's your problem?"

"He is mad," Dolly says, "he gives me the creeps. He is a bad influence on Tommy. He supplies *hadia* to my son on the sly, just to spite me."

"Ha ha!" Madho chuckles. "As if Tommy *needs* any prodding. But that's not the point, my darling Dolly*ji*. I need his money to put into our kitty for a house. If we throw him out, we will have practically no savings. I am almost there—another year and I will have saved enough to allow me to approach a bank for a housing loan. That is, if the company doesn't throw *bhaiyya* out before that. If only I could get one *lakh* rupees from somewhere . . . Then I could go to a bank right away."

"*Khayali pulav*, Madho *buddhu!*" Dolly says endearingly, enjoying the drift of the conversation and caressing her husband's thighs seductively.

"No—no, Dolly*ji*," Madho protests, aroused and high, "just you wait and watch! You will have a palace of your own soon, and you will rule there like a queen."

"*Baba?*" Tina asks timorously, coming out of the children's bedroom. "C-can I watch the ten o'clock news?"

"Why?" Madho asks gruffly. "Have you finished your diet of books for the evening? Can't you see we are watching TV? Go eat your dinner and sleep. And where is Mona? Ask her if she wants to watch this show."

"*B-b-Baba,* Mona has g-gone to a f-friend's place. Sh-she will return only after d-dinner."

"What?" Madho screams, as if Tina is to blame for her sister's impropriety. "With whose permission?"

"Come on, Madho, *I* sent her," Dolly says imperiously. "She was feeling so bored at home, I gave her some money to go to the movies with her friends and have dinner at Rebecca's. Hope you don't mind?"

"Oh! That's all right, then. Mama's pet, is she? And you, stupid girl—learn something from your *ma* and *didi.* There is more to life than books and music. At least comb your hair in the evenings, for God's sake! Now have your dinner in the kitchen, and leave us in peace. And fetch us a bottle of chilled water from the fridge after you have finished."

Crestfallen and hurt, Tina scampers into the tiny kitchen. She rummages through the ancient refrigerator and takes out some rice and vegetable curry. Dolly has cooked fish, but Tina isn't going to risk getting hauled up for being greedy by eating it before everyone else has had dinner. She can eat any leftovers the following day. She mixes her rice and curry together and heats it in a pan. She ladles the hot gruel onto her steel plate and dumps in a couple of green chilies. She loves hot chilies. They singe her tongue and make her eyes smart; she can't have a meal without them. Her stepmother says it is another unhealthy trait in her.

Tina opens the back door and goes out onto the small veranda behind the kitchen. She sits on a wooden stool she keeps there and eats quietly. She likes sitting here. Rarely does anyone bother her out here. And if someone needs her, she can easily hear their shouts through the kitchen door.

Tina is wearing an oversize faded cotton frock with a blueberry print. As she bends over the plate in her lap, her straight, tangled hair cascades along her cheeks, threatening to get into the food. She eats deftly and hungrily with her brown fingers and stuffs big morsels into her mouth. Through the tangle of hair, her eyes flash brilliantly in the dark, almost like a cat's. They are big, alert, and intelligent—timid and defiant at the same time. She pauses to shake back her hair from her eyes.

She looks up at the overcast sky and wonders what the hidden stars are doing. She wonders if it is true that after death, good souls become stars and watch over their loved ones below. If so, she is certain that on most nights, her departed mother must be looking down at her as she sits on the veranda. She bites into the chili and convinces herself that the tears in her eyes are from the hot stuff.

No one understands her except her *kaku,* Raimoti. She is so alone, so secluded. How she sometimes wishes to end this life of misery and humiliation. But she knows that the only way out for her is to study, get a job, and move out.

She wants to be an engineer. She used to have a neighbor, a girl about four years older, who performed so well on the board exams that the company funded the engineering course for which she qualified through an entrance examination. Tina's teachers and friends are unanimous in their view that she is far superior to that girl. Tina's principal has already spoken to the chairman of the company, who has promised that if the girl qualifies on the test, the company will fund her studies. It would be an excellent weapon against labor unions, who constantly clamor for greater welfare measures. Funding one student through a government engineering college is relatively cheap but has high publicity value—it will grab headlines, get coverage on the local cable network, and come to the notice of prominent social workers and local authorities.

At thirteen, Tina is grown up beyond her years. At the age when most little girls are learning to fold their own clothes, Tina often cooks meals for everyone at home. Somehow Mona always manages to escape that task. Increasingly, Tina is saddled with household chores and responsibilities. For some strange reason, her stepmother dislikes her and treats her more as house help than as a child. Equally inexplicably, her father lets Dolly do this.

It was not always like this. Although Tina's mother died when she was under five, the girl still carries many good memories of infancy. There was a time when she felt loved and cared for, when she did not feel that growing up was painful.

She was her mother's favorite. She remembers being patted to sleep with her mother humming soft lullabies in her ears. Although Tina has forgotten the meaningless jumble of baby words, the tune is still fresh in her mind. Sometimes she hums it for herself and invents new rhymes to fit the tune. Once she gathered the courage to sing it for Mona, hoping that her sister might remember the lullaby, too. But Mona just laughed derisively and told Tina that it sounded like a donkey with a stick up its arse. Only Raimoti, when he heard her accidentally one day, called her aside and stared long and deep into her timid eyes. "Like a runaway kite," he said at long last, patting her affectionately before walking away. Tina didn't quite understand what he meant but felt a warm glow at being noticed and appreciated.

Her uncle is like this. He creates mysteries around him. As he has grown older, he seems less and less connected with the world around him. It wasn't so bad when Tina was a little girl. She remembers that he assembled a crude swing for her with some old planks and strung it from a big tree across the street. She loved it and spent hours on it on empty afternoons after school. At times he would come to her with small gifts—a packet of toffees or a ripe mango or a spinning top. Once he brought her a bicycle chain. Very often there was no apparent logic to his gifts, but Tina always felt the warmth with which they were given and cherished whatever he gave her. She has a small, dented aluminum trunk where she still keeps a collection of his odd offerings and feels that each item must have meant something for her uncle—only she can't figure out what.

It isn't as if Raimoti is always there for her. He could vanish for days without a word to anyone. Then, one fine morning, they would all wake up to his powerful voice singing in the courtyard outside, oblivious to Dolly's noisy disapproval and Madho's pleadings. Sometimes he would call Tina aside and inquire about her school and studies and look pleased when she told him about some recent academic achievement. But on many days Tina finds it impossible to draw his attention. He would move around in a trance, ignoring her and everyone around, mumbling under his breath and staring into the sky.

But all the while Tina somehow knows that if there is one person with whom she connects or of whom she can ask anything, it is her uncle. He never says no to her. When she reached sixth grade, she needed a geometry set. Her father was inclined to buy one, but Dolly convinced him that Tina could use one of the old sets that Mona discarded. Tina had been disappointed. The protractor was cracked, and the compass had a bent point. She still doesn't know how Raimoti came to know of it, but the next day, when she returned from school, she found a shiny new geometry set lying on her stool on the veranda behind the kitchen.

Raimoti is a reassuring if a little unreliable presence in Tina's life. She doesn't know why, she is just happy knowing.

Tina finishes her meal and goes into the kitchen to wash her plate. Thankfully, her parents have hired a part-time maid who comes in twice a day to sweep and to clean utensils. But out of habit, Tina always washes her own plate, and if the maid doesn't turn up, she is expected to clean others', too.

She peeps out of the kitchen to check on what her father and stepmother are doing. She finds them still watching TV and is relieved to note that there is some water left in the glass jug on the wobbly coffee table in the sitting room. They haven't missed her yet.

Tina wipes her hands dry on the gaudy silver-and-red curtain sagging from a wire above the kitchen door. Dolly bought it as a classy interior-decoration intervention, and whenever no one is looking, Tina wipes her hands on it. She knows that it is difficult to pinpoint her because both Mona and her stepbrother, Tommy, do it openly and frequently, despite remonstrations from Dolly. It is a dangerous thing to do, but Tina is very careful, and it gives her a small measure of unholy delight.

Mona and Tommy do some other forbidden things that Tina is only beginning to fully understand. She keeps quiet about them and tries to ignore them. She is a pragmatic girl and knows what can get her into trouble with people. Lately, she has discovered that keeping secrets also empowers. Occasionally, she can extract some favors out of Mona if she hints at knowing things that their father ought to know but doesn't. Tina knows that is not very ethical but is gradually learning to use every tiny weapon and ruse to survive. She is growing into a tactical fighter. She has to—there is no one else to fight for her.

Tina takes out a bottle of water from the fridge. Then she removes a tray of ice cubes and empties it into a plastic bowl. She picks them up and pushes Dolly's curtain aside with her waiflike shoulders to enter the sitting room.

The tableau of cozy domestic peace is shattered by a frenzied knock on the door. Tina hurriedly puts the bowl of ice on the table and rushes to open it, still holding the bottle of water in her hand. A colleague of her father's tumbles in, out of breath and ashen.

"Mine Number Three has been breached!" he announces. "Your brother Raimoti is still trapped inside. Everyone is rushing to the site, Madho. Come on, let's go! Water is gushing in from the lake with great force—there is very little time—hurry!"

The bottle slips from Tina's hand and crashes on the cement floor, sending a great splash of broken glass and water across the room.

chapter 4

The cold, sinewy paw shatters through the roughblack membrane of the mine and gropes for a tentative foothold on the quivering floor.

Inches away, Arif is a statue, arms frozen still in the downward swing of his pickax, eyes wide open with fear, lips parted in an unuttered yell.

Raimoti, lurking a step behind, slowly stands erect, clutching at a cold crowbar. Another loud crack, another rent, and the second paw breaks out. Then a third. A paw to find them, another to rule over them, and a third to crush them all and bind them in the darkness. Raimoti recognizes the looming shadow of his Beast. The eternal wait is over. This is the moment of reckoning that he has dreaded for aeons; this is the moment of confrontation he has replayed a thousand times in his mind. This is it. Time stands still.

Everything fades into a whirlpool of darkness with only the Beast in the vortex. It and him. Circling in an ever narrowing gyre. The oth-

ers are mere props—foot soldiers. The puddle flowers into a pond, the pond into a rivulet. The rivulet becomes a raging river. The river becomes an ocean of fear. They are engulfed. Engulfed and overwhelmed. Is there a way out?

There is an eternity of benumbing shock. A momentary lapse of animation. Arif stares in horror at the icy jets gushing out from the coal face, recoiling as if from venomous snakes. Foamyblack water curls around their ankles, sending a chill up their spines—grabbing, slithering, and licking. Birsa, the young buck, feels the gorge rise in his throat and ducks behind the rickety wheelbarrow in an instinctive though futile attempt to put something, anything, between him and the charging Beast. They feel a dry hopelessness clutching their hearts—a hopelessness that only a miner can feel, buried hundreds of feet below the surface, watching deadly water fill all the space, pushing out air, swamping life.

"Run," Raimoti commands in a quiet voice. "We don't have much time. We have to reach the upper level before this tunnel gets completely flooded. I don't know if there is another breach on that level—in which case we are doomed. But if not, we can try to take the cage lift to Entrance Number One from there."

Mine Number 3 is an old mine. It has only two shaft openings: one with a small, open lift—often called a cage—to transport men and small quantities of coal, and another, larger one, called a skip. The skip shaft goes all the way down to the lowest of the three levels of the mine—to Level 1—while the cage shaft goes down only to the uppermost, Level 3.

"Don't be crazy, *kaka,*" Birsa rebuts. "There is a shaft landing for Entrance Number Two on this level, and it has a bigger skip instead of a cage. We would be much better off heading toward that."

"I know that, Birsa. But remember, the skip landing is at a lower height than here and it might get flooded much quicker. If we get trapped there, it won't be possible for us to retrace our steps against the force of the water, and attempt to reach the upper level. No, we should just head straight for the cage lift."

Had Bibhash been present, he would have tiredly explained to Birsa that most old underground mines have at least two entry or exit points. Apart from functional expediency, they serve as respiratory canals for the mines. Deep under the surface, ventilation is a major concern for engineers. Improper or inadequate ventilation can result in serious operational problems and might even cause dangerous accidents, because underground coal mining releases large quantities of coal-bed methane, a potentially flammable gas. Mining also produces coal dust, which is also prone to spontaneous combustion. Therefore, mining engineers take all precautions to keep the presence of these two by-products well within acceptable levels. Miners are extremely alert to any increase in these lethal elements underground. Till not very long ago, they would carry a small bird in a cage to monitor the presence of poisonous methane by observing its effect on the bird—the canary in the mine—and make divinations from the asphyxiation of the canary. In many places, they carried a small lamp, and the color and flicker of the flame would warn an experienced miner about any increase in the proportion of dangerous gases. With time, newer and more sophisticated devices have replaced the canary and the flame, but airflow remains a very crucial factor in an underground mine.

Raimoti knows that he and his gang are working in the extreme eastern corner of Level 2 and that the coal seam slopes down from east to west. He also knows that the cage shaft has a landing on Level 3, not very far from the eastern boundary of the mine, while the skip shaft is situated almost toward the western limit, with landings on each of the three levels.

Inclines, synclines, gradients, all very technical terms, but Raimoti has worked long enough burrowing into the earth and has a remarkably intuitive grasp of the layouts of mines. The skip shaft lies to their west, where all the water is flowing. He reckons that by the time they traverse the maze of corridors to the western end, the lowest level of the mine will almost certainly be flooded. That would mean that the tail-end pulley for the skip would be submerged under several thousand cubic meters of water. The winding mechanisms will break down. If they are foolish enough to attempt an escape via the skip, they will probably find themselves stranded on a lower plane, with the only exit blocked off.

There is another thought that bothers Raimoti: every underground mine has some natural amount of persistent flooding due to seepage of groundwater. Mine Number 3 has a greater than average amount of seepage due to its proximity to the lake. To counter this, the mine engineers have fitted it with four heavy-duty pumps: two on Level 1 and one each on Levels 2 and 3. Water from each level goes into specially designed channels and conduits and collects at a sump next to the tail-end pulley of the skip shaft. From there, two powerful pumps raise the water half a kilometer up to the surface, where it is led off into drains. Levels 2 and 3 have smaller pumps to be used for localized seepage and for emergencies such as this. But the problem lies in the fact that the pumps on Level 1 are the oldest and therefore the least reliable.

Worse still is the fact that the main switchboard for the mine's internal power distribution is located next to the Level 1 sump. It will be the first to short-circuit in the event of flooding on Level 1. That will mean instantaneous collapse of the lighting and communication network. Thankfully, the Level 1 cage is powered through a switchboard on the surface. Though working their way up to Level 3 might take them longer, the chances of finding a working lift would be much higher. Also, if the pumps fail, it will take much longer to flood Level 3—unless, of course, there has been a breach at that level, too. But there is little anyone can do about that. So Raimoti is quite sure: they must set out for the cage landing on Level 3. And fast. Raimoti knows there is only one way to escape the Beast—to outrun it.

Birsa, the young rebel, has other ideas. He thinks a skip is far sturdier than a cage and therefore more dependable. He knows that the skip shaft is an inlet for fresh air, so the air in its vicinity will be purer than that near the cage shaft. Also, the intercom lines come in along the skip shaft, and there is an instrument at every landing. In the worst-case scenario, they can request a lifeline to be dropped down. It will be very slow and cumbersome, but it has been done in the past. If, as Raimoti says, they head for Level 3, and if, as he fears, there is a breach on that level as well, they might find themselves cut off completely from the surface. Birsa feels any rescue attempt can only be made through the skip shaft, which is wider.

"I place my trust in Raimoti's judgment," Arif declares, deciding for everyone. "He is the most experienced, and he knows his way around. Let's head for the cage shaft on Level Three."

Birsa tries to argue, but the men, led by Arif, have already started trotting toward the connection to the corridor leading to the main tunnel, which reaches Level 3. They pay no attention to Birsa. Stickyblack water is rising rapidly around their knees, trying to suck them down. Birsa never imagined how quickly a mine would flood. Within moments, water has risen above their knees, and with every second, it is rising higher. He feels breathless and caged in. Most horrifying is the ominous thunder of the water pouring into the mine. It sweeps over his senses, and he feels his faculties drowning in the deluge. Reluctantly, he follows the others. There is no time to waste.

Birsa is no coward, but he is no coal miner, either. As he plods through the suffocating corridors, he curses the circumstances that have thrown him in this job and now into this horrid situation. When he thinks of it, he has made many wrong decisions in his life—some that he can even call blunders, in retrospect. But the worst of them all was his impulsive decision to come to these wretched pits.

Unlike most of his coworkers, he is neither very poor nor uneducated. His father was a postman, a well-respected and honorable position in their remote forest village. His family owned three acres of land, more than enough to feed them. Birsa was the youngest of two brothers and two sisters. His father brought them up well: he educated his sons and married off his daughters to good families from the towns. After finishing high school, Birsa's older brother was sent off to the nearest university town for college education. As expected, he picked up a job there and pulled himself out of the rut of rural existence.

By the time Birsa finished his schooling, his father had retired. There was less disposable income, and the family needed a young male to look after the fields. At that time, Birsa thought that he preferred being a farmer to working for someone in the town. He had a proud nature and a free spirit. The decision suited everybody.

Relieved, his old man handed over most of the responsibilities to Birsa and devoted himself to his long-cherished dream of writing his family's history, which everyone knew would be of no interest to anyone else. Being one of the few people from his tribe who had stuck to the old religion and not gotten converted by zealous missionaries, he was also a devout man. Whatever spare time he had was spent in prayers and rituals. His wife, a quiet and docile woman, ran the home efficiently and prudently so that her husband did not have to seek a part-time job after retirement.

Birsa surprised himself and his parents—who still thought of him as the baby of the family—by turning around their modest farm. He hired labor intelligently, got better-quality seeds for free from government agencies, procured subsidized fertilizer from the state warehouse, and changed the crop pattern in his fields. He put to good use his native intelligence, aggression, and education. At sixteen, he was the smartest farmer in the village.

His first harvest brought such good yield that for the first time in their memory, they had a surplus that they could sell in the local wholesale markets for a neat profit. He bought a gold nose stud for his mother and a wristwatch for his father.

They didn't say anything to him but preened when the neighbors praised their son.

But the next crop season was a bad one in that province. The monsoons failed to water the crops, and several families were reduced to penury. Only his father's pension, his mother's economy, his brother's contributions, and Birsa's undying labor kept them afloat. All around them, loans mounted, and when banks refused them, people turned to local loan sharks. The result was disastrous for most.

In Birsa's village alone, eight farmers committed suicide, leaving behind helpless wives and children or aged parents. State officials and politicians came, made promises and speeches, and left. Slick journalists with cameras and sunglasses interviewed the mourning families, took videos and photographs, and left. Incensed social workers wearing *khadi* and subtle perfumes ranted, raved, instigated, and left.

In the end it was just the villagers, their hunger, and their grief. And mounting anger at their own helplessness.

That was when the first band of young robbers formed. When they couldn't earn bread, they learned to loot. No trader, moneylender, or landlord was safe. No one knew how, but soon the angry young men started getting supplies of modern arms—rifles, explosives, and grenades. Someone taught them how to make Molotov cocktails and guns out of bicycle rods. Clandestine political overtures were made, and huge sums of cash poured in. No one cared or understood the motives of those strategists.

When the village acquired sufficient notoriety, the men in khaki came in jeeps and raided homes. Thankfully, not too many women and girls were raped, but some old men were killed in fake encounters. Instead of discouraging the bands of militant youth, the police inflamed them into committing more daring acts.

Through all this, Birsa remained focused on his land and responsibilities. In that second year of farming, he still managed to avoid loans. It was the third year that put him up against the wall.

For the second year in a row, the monsoons failed. The district was officially declared drought-stricken. More farmers killed themselves, and at times their families joined them in the great escape. The only solution that presented itself was to mortgage half the land to the local bank and take a loan to dig a tube well. The manager knew Birsa's father, and the loan got processed with speed and very little extra expenditure. They all heaved a sigh of relief. They believed that statistically, the rain gods could not fail them a third year and that they would be able to pay back the loans.

Having given up on government, politicians, bureaucrats, journalists, and nongovernmental organizations the villagers turned to the only hope they had left: they prayed to the rain gods for a bumper monsoon. They were not disappointed—the gods did not neglect the village the following year. It poured. The heavens burst open, and there was a deluge such as no one remembered. Standing crops were washed away almost overnight. Bunds and culverts were destroyed. *Kuccha,* or mud houses, were obliterated. Cattle and poultry drowned, and rotting carcasses floated in the submerged fields, giving out putrid fumes and inviting vermin and vultures, not to mention big men in helicopters. For twelve days, Birsa and his parents were forced to live on their terrace because their house was flooded. If there was a hell without fire, it was there.

After a week of death and destruction, the army was called in to deliver relief. The choppers dropped food, utensils, and blankets on starving and crazed people who rushed out to stand under the flying machines. When four children and three adults were crushed to death under the dropped packages, the army withdrew airborne relief. They switched to motorized rubber rafts and were beaten, bruised, and robbed by marooned villagers. After two days, all relief work stopped. Thankfully, the rains stopped, too.

It took a fortnight for the water to drain out of the fields, leaving behind decay and epidemic. Birsa's mother fell sick with cholera and pulmonary effusion. The doctors sent by the state administration to deliver free medical aid and supplies instead black-marketed the drugs they were meant to give away. Soon Birsa and his father had nothing left. Birsa's brother came to visit and left behind all his savings, but that was not enough for either their mother's treatment or repairs to the house. Finally, Birsa's father was compelled to approach a moneylender. Their home was mortgaged. The next day Birsa's mother passed away. The money borrowed for her treatment came in handy for her funeral.

Slowly, life started to return to normal. Grief, like happiness, isn't eternal. Birsa's father had aged a hundred years in those few weeks, but he lived. It isn't all that easy to die while one lives. Birsa put all his energies into rebuilding their house and reviving his farm. Life started to stabilize.

Then the bank and the moneylender attacked them in unison. After the floods, the old manager had taken a transfer, and the new manager was a true professional who wanted to collect all dues. The moneylender was even more enthusiastic. The bank fixed a date for the auction of their fields, and the moneylender gave them the option of buying their house if they didn't repay the loan in a month.

Birsa had never felt like drinking liquor before, but the evening when the bank served its notice, he sought out some old friends from school, and they bought a few bottles of country-brewed liquor made from fermented oranges. He drank through the night and was astonished to find a simple solution to his problems: his friends confided that they were members of the local branch of the People's Soldiers and that they would be happy to help him.

Two nights later, they assembled in the scrubland on the outskirts of the village to fortify themselves for the task ahead. Birsa was accompanied by half a dozen People's Soldiers to the moneylender's house. His friends were all armed to the teeth and had even given him a country-made pistol—a *katta*.

Unfortunately, the moneylender was prepared for such eventualities and tried to scare them off with his double-barrel. Birsa's *katta* went off in his hand, and the man died on the spot. On the advice of his friends, to avoid any witnesses, Birsa also shot dead the moneylender's wife and two children. Then they ransacked the house and took away all the cash they found. His friends took half, and Birsa carried the rest back to his father.

The old man was sitting by a small fire in the courtyard of their dilapidated house. He heard Birsa's story with little expression and accepted the bundle. Then he dumped it in the fire before his son's disbelieving eyes.

Sometimes sons feel hate and respect together for their fathers. Birsa did that night.

He ran away into the hills to a hidden camp of the People's Soldiers. When he heard that his father had been implicated and arrested for conspiring to kill the moneylender, Birsa felt shame but could not find the courage to surrender to the police. Instead, he chose to run—away from life as he had known it and into a life that would hide him forever. There was nothing left for him to go back to.

Birsa was asked by the camp commandant to leave so as not to jeopardize his comrades. For months he roamed the countryside like a vagabond, earning a living doing hard labor, when he could find work, and stealing when he couldn't. He felt betrayed by friends who had promised to help him, betrayed by his father who had spurned his help, and betrayed by his own soul that could not sleep in peace with his body. His embittered mind had no love, no faith, and no patience left in it, and he despised any form of authority. His heart was always so full of emotions that he started burning them with hatred. This furnace sought fuel that he'd found in the underground coal mines of Kariakhani six months before. It was a fine place for simmering hearts and people who didn't want to be found.

Only he hadn't expected water in a furnace. One flood had taken enough out of his life. He could not face another. He had come here seeking absolution, not death. He is scared. Water scares him.

An underground mine is a labyrinth of tunnels designed to reach every remote foot of the coal seam. Despite their geometric pattern, or perhaps because of it, they can be confounding in their complexity. There are markers and glow signs to guide people, but these are mostly for the benefit of the *sahib* log—the guide system for elite engineers and managers, who seldom descend to those depths. The miners rely largely on their senses to guide them through the labyrinth.

Those who have had the opportunity to go river-rafting down a gushing Himalayan rapid might be able to imagine the sheer power of a water current. But even they would not be able to fully comprehend the impact such a rapid might have two hundred feet below the surface of earth, in the jet-black craters of a coal mine. There is only water, diminishing air, and blackness.

Raimoti is the Lord of Blackness. He brandishes his crowbar above his head as he rushes forward, away from the gaping mouth of the Beast, his spindly legs pumping relentlessly under his frail body, rising knee-high and splashing down into the inky stream. Arif allows him to move to the front of their column as he tears down the winding corridors, now turning left at a corner, now right, now up an incline. They follow him blindly, hurtling in his delirious wake.

Suddenly, the dim overhead electric lamps flicker, a sign that water has poured down to the switchboard on Level 1 below. There is a bright flash as a surge of electricity goes through the circuit, and then the corridor is plunged into utter darkness. A distant boom echoes through the tunnel, signaling the crash of the transformer. Raimoti skids to a halt, and Arif collides into him. The others, following a little behind, also come to a halt, each man marked by the glimmer of his headlamp. Even Raimoti is lost. He stands there, panting and peering into the gloom, water lapping almost at his waist.

For what seems like an eternity, they stand without uttering a word. They feel the gush of water more than see it. The darkness is thick and humid, and it drapes around them like a shroud, stifling and oppressive. The headlamps are mere flickers bobbing on a river of death.

"Which way now?" Birsa inquires derisively, as if it is all Raimoti's fault.

"Can't say. Let me think."

"Sure, think! While we all drown here—*saala ganjedi!* Bloody drug addict!"

"All right," Raimoti replies with a sigh, "we continue up this corridor till we reach the next intersection, then we take a right. From what I can guess, we should be approaching the cage shaft from the west. That means we have to turn right, and after reaching the main tunnel, turn back left—that should take us close to the cage landing on Level Three."

"Wonderful!" Birsa retorts with sarcasm, addressing Lakhan and Sagan, lost boys who always tried to be his friends, impressed by his savage nature. "The old fool wants us to trust his rotting brain and follow his directions—as if things are not bad enough already. Hey, *Bhagwan*! Oh God! What a mess!"

"Look, Birsa," Raimoti says tiredly, "I am doing the best I can. I think I remember the way. I could be mistaken, of course, but I don't think so. I have a feeling that we are moving in the right direction. In any case, I don't think anyone here is too certain. So just let me lead the way till we reach the main corridor. Then we can decide."

"I think Raimoti is right," Arif says firmly. "This is no place to argue; we are too close to the breach. We should get as far away from it as quickly as possible. We will reassess the direction once we reach the main corridor."

"Right," Birsa bridles, "but the point is whether this crazy man can take us to the main corridor at all. I doubt it very much."

"Well, can you take us there? Can you guarantee that?" Arif hisses, turning upon Birsa in anger.

Birsa lapses into a sullen silence. He is too new here to really know his way around. He just doesn't want to accept Raimoti as the leader. Always having to listen to Arif is bad enough, but to have this ganja addict bossing him around is absolutely intolerable. He can make an intelligent guess about the direction, but he cannot risk guaranteeing anything. He knows that if they get lost along the way—which, under the circumstances, is not too unlikely—there will be hell to pay. Arif won't forgive him.

"Because if not," growls Arif, as if hearing his thoughts, "you better shut up and let Raimoti lead. If you want us to follow you, be very careful. If you get us lost, I will bust your fucking head with my pickax."

Birsa hates Arif. True, Arif is more experienced and a natural leader, but he is too arrogant. He can't tolerate differences of opinion and likes to bulldoze his way through. These are exactly the traits that Birsa has. Maybe the two of them are too similar to get along.

Then there is the matter of Arif's religion. Birsa is a devout
Hindu and worships Hanuman with a passion. Religion was the
one influence from his father that he hasn't been able to discard.
To be subordinate to a Muslim like Arif is humiliating for him. It's
not even as if Arif is superior in rank—they are both workmen—so
why should he accept Arif as his boss? And there is something very
fishy about the strange rapport Arif shares with Raimoti. It is disgusting how the two stick to each other. Not only does one have to
show deference to Arif, one also has to be polite to the lunatic. On
many occasions Birsa has tried to rope in the support of Lakhan
and Sagan against Arif—both hailing from his region and belong-
ing to the same community—but they are too young and timid.
They don't want to risk a confrontation with Arif, who has a nasty
record of violence. Birsa will have to bide his time and wait for the
right moment to strike.

Raimoti turns around and shuffles ahead, using his crowbar
as a blind man would use his walking stick. Arif and the rest follow
him down the corridor. Birsa, humiliated and fuming, falls in line,
and they trudge through the darkness with only the murkyellow
glow from their headlamps to guide them. The splashing roar of
water has subsided into a dull, gushing sound—an indicator that
the narrow tunnel where they were working has been completely
inundated and the point of breach has submerged. The relative
silence is even scarier. Birsa recites the *Hanuman Chalisa* under
his breath. He trips over a submerged outcropping of rock, and his
voice rises involuntarily in volume, carrying shrilly over the dull
rumble of water.

"Yes, right!" Arif calls from the front of the column with a laugh. "Call upon your monkey god to help us—he might understand your language."

Birsa gets a sudden urge to run up and smash his shovel over the bastard's head. He makes an impulsive move but finds Lakhan's restraining hand on his shoulder. He swallows his rage and continues in silence. He is fast reaching a flash point.

Negotiating the narrow corridors of a coal mine is always a treacherous proposition. Doing so in utter darkness is almost suicidal. Walking through a pitch-dark coal mine in knee-deep churning water is insanity. But Raimoti is quite comfortable with that. He shuts his eyes and abandons himself to pure instinct. His boots slither tentatively like crabs over the bumpy surface, feeling outcrops of rock, shallows, and cracks: each wary step a torturous journey.

To move up to Level 3 from Level 2, he must first proceed toward Entrance Number 2, to the west. He must keep the air current in his face. Once he reaches a cross-current, he must turn his back to the breeze and head east to Entrance Number 1. He moves like a man in trance, nostrils flaring to catch the tiniest whiff of air, ears twitching nervously to detect the slightest change in the pitch or tone of the surrounding rumble. The others follow him blindly with an occasional curse as someone trips or slips.

Raimoti sucks on a bittersweet lump of bhang that he always carries in a small pouch hidden inside his baggy trousers. It is potent—he made it from handpicked weeds—and it melts slowly in his mouth. Time is a state of mind, Raimoti realizes—how strange!

Our happiest moments are just that—moments. Our saddest

hours are eternities. Happiness, fear, sorrow, pain are all emotions that mold, edit, and quantify time. Our actions also influence time. Hang from a cliff and time stands still. Meet a dear friend after many years and time flies. Walk down a coal mine getting flooded and discover limbo. Swallow a ball of bhang and experience fluctuating eternity.

He also carries a small *chillum*, a matchbox, and some ganja wrapped in a polyethylene packet. But now is not the time for such luxuries.

Raimoti feels the wall breathing heavily, crowding in on him. He pushes with his right hand, then slams his crowbar into the wall. The wall grudgingly moves away, allowing him to go deeper into the darkness, pulling his ragged team by the quivering beams of their headlamps.

He parts the thickblack foliage of fear and comes to a halt. The beams fan out around him like the wings of a dying eagle. The wings flutter, flap, and then burst into a thousand shards of glittering glass, piercing his skin like a hundred needles. He shivers, and the shards rain down to collect as shimmering foam around his feet. There is only a soft breeze caressing his face to remind him of the broken wings.

The breeze reverses its direction and then changes back. It is a cross-current!

"I think we have reached the intersection," Raimoti says, peering into the gloom.

Arif takes a few steps to the left and touches a wall. Then he turns and walks to the opposite wall. "Ten paces," he declares. "This must be the main corridor. I think we take a left from here— right? *Kaka? Kaka?* Are you okay?"

"Shhh!" Raimoti cocks his head to one side.

"What? What is it?"

"The bastard must be hallucinating again, Arif—let's proceed," Birsa says impatiently, pushing ahead.

"Quiet—listen!" Raimoti whispers.

"What is it, *kaka*? Don't freak us out, please," Arif implores.

"Do you hear the rumble?"

"Yes, of course. It's coming from behind us. It's the water."

"No, not this one. It's coming from our left—from the east end. Listen carefully."

They huddle together and listen. They are caught in a complex web of sound: a heavy strand of dull rumbles and drones, sharp strands of cracks and creaks. The fine mesh of sound drapes around them, trapping them in its center. There are echoes and reverberations, making it impossible to figure out the noise's direction. But yes, there is a new rumble, which seems to be rising above the rest like a crescendo of drums in a symphony.

"Ye-es . . . I think I can hear it. What is it, *kaka*?" Arif asks, swallowing hard, trying not to think about the possibilities.

"What? What can you hear?" Birsa shouts, turning upon Arif. "There is nothing, do you understand? Nothing! Now don't let us waste any more time, let's turn left—toward the cage landing."

The Beast has many heads—like Ravana, the ten-headed demon lord. It has many paws, too. Raimoti hears the stealthy slither of newer paws approaching from the east. The Beast is crafty but not enough to fool Raimoti.

The low sound is camouflaged but unmistakable. The Beast has breached another entry. There is water pouring into Level 3 now.

"We can't go to the cage landing now," Raimoti observes

dully. "That part is flooding, too. We have to turn right—toward
the skip landing—and take our chances."

"What?" Birsa shouts incredulously. "Now that we have found
the main corridor, you want us to go back west and walk almost
two kilometers to the skip landing? You really *are* crazy, Raimoti. If
you wanted us to take the skip, we could have done so from Level
Two. First we wasted time climbing up from Level Two, and now
you want us to waste more time by walking back the whole length
of the mine to the west end? You will kill us, you lunatic!"

"Birsa, *beta,* I wanted to take us to the cage, but I am sure I
can hear a fresh breach in that direction. Remember? The lake is
to the east of the mine. Obviously, the cracks on the lower level
have expanded vertically. If we turn left, we will be walking into
the flow of water."

"Water?" Birsa asks, pale with rising fear. "What water? There
is no water here. Can't you see? Are you fucking blind? The corridor is dry!"

"Oh? And don't you feel the puff of breeze coming from the
left?" Raimoti asks.

"I don't. And even if you do, what is your point, you madman? Don't you know there is a cage shaft at the end of the corridor? It is probably just an air drift from that shaft."

"No, Birsa," Raimoti says, shaking his head grimly. "Even a
new hand like you must know that these tunnels are ventilated
so that air flows in from the west—from the skip shaft—and out
from the cage shaft in the east. There are no reversions of this airflow. You can feel a light drift only if you are within a few meters
of the cage shaft. But we must be at least half a kilometer from the

shaft. The breeze I feel on my face is quite steady and strong, and it is coming from the wrong direction."

"Oh! Really? Then I guess someone is farting near the cage landing, right? Is that your explanation, Raimoti?"

"The explanation is," says Raimoti, "that water is displacing air. Water is coming into the tunnel with such force that it is pushing air back against the flow. I have heard of such a phenomenon. My grandfather warned me of it."

"Great!" Birsa grunts in exasperation. "As if it isn't bad enough having a lunatic like you guide us, now you are bringing in your dead grandfather, you son of a whore!"

"Don't get abusive, Birsa—Raimoti is only doing his best to get us out," Arif intervenes.

"Why?" Birsa shouts, whipping around. "Are you the only one with the right to abuse? You circumcised pig! And why do you feel so worked up? Was your mother a whore?"

Before anyone can react, Arif crashes into Birsa, throwing him to the floor. They roll a few times and come up against the wall. Arif straddles Birsa's chest and grabs his hair, banging his head down on the black rocks. For a few seconds, Birsa is paralyzed into inaction—he hadn't expected this onslaught. He lies there like a rag doll, groaning under the painful badgering. But all miners have a strong survival instinct, and that instinct takes over now.

With a scream, Birsa drives a wicked fist into Arif's face, which is contorted in violence. Birsa's fist crashes into the unprotected face with a sickening crunch, and Arif's nose starts bleeding. The punch has knocked Arif back, and Birsa rises into a half-sitting position. He picks up a small lump of coal and smashes it down on

Arif's head. With a groan, Arif falls away from Birsa; before he can get up, Birsa gets to his feet and starts kicking his fallen adversary in the stomach with a mad fury. Arif is bleeding profusely from his nose and can't breathe too well. He tries to grab the flaying legs, but Birsa's kicks are like pistons.

Raw violence benumbs those who are watching; it has that petrifying effect on most people. It is almost hypnotizing. This violence has to be distinguished from the structured violence that we see in boxing matches or *corrida de toros* bullfights. No matter how desperate the structured fight, we know that it is a sport. We might even feel thrilled by the show of violence. But those of us who have had the misfortune of witnessing an act of raw violence know that when the sole aim of a fight is to kill, there is no thrill, no fun—it only gives one a dry, sinking feeling. There is something very intimidating and repulsive in seeing any life fight for its survival, be it the mouse against the cat or one man against another. Such raw violence transforms itself into a virtual beast, and we either flee from it or lapse into absolute stillness, so as not to draw its attention.

Raimoti watches with dilated pupils the writhing and moaning creature rolling about on the floor of the mine, now becoming one body, now splitting in two. Pummeling hands sprout from where there should be legs, flailing legs unfurl from between heads. Stomachs split apart to show contorted faces that scream, spit, and bite. Raimoti is transfixed for a moment, watching the horrifying antics of this violent animal. Then the bigger horror of a deadlier Beast recalls him to his senses, and he leaps onto the writhing mass of limbs.

Today Raimoti is invincible. Nothing can stand in his way. He grabs a leg of the animal bucking around him and sinks his teeth deep into flesh. There is a howl, but Raimoti presses on and grabs a fistful of hair, yanking till his fingers pull out a tuft. He impales his scrawny body between the heaving twin stomachs of the wild creature and pushes with all his might till the creature tears apart, howling in shocked agony. For a few moments Raimoti, Arif, and Birsa lie panting on the floor.

"Enough!" Raimoti grunts. "I won't have any more of this foolishness. We are trying to save ourselves, not kill each other. Stop this right now, or else I shall have to kill you."

Raimoti has the reputation of someone who is not all there. He is commonly perceived as a slightly crazy old man who hovers on the edge of some unreal world, entering into the real one only intermittently. But everyone has heard the hushed stories of his latent violence. He seems to have little respect for life—or rather, life and death don't hold the same significance for him as they do for ordinary people. The most famous legend tells of a miner who tried to molest Raimoti's niece Tina. After a few weeks, the man went missing. This was common enough in the coal mines, where migrant labor came and went. People had almost forgotten the man when his body was found at the bottom of a long-abandoned pit. The body was so broken that it could barely be recognized. It was dismissed as an accident, but people wondered. They didn't like to push Raimoti beyond a point.

Panting and bruised, Birsa gets to his feet, refusing to look at anybody. Quietly, he picks up his helmet and shovel. For a long moment he stands there, his head hanging. Finally, he turns to his supporters, Lakhan and Sagan. "If you want to stay with these raving lunatics, do so. But they will kill you before you can get out. If you want to save yourselves, come with me."

Birsa turns on his heel and walks into the corridor to the left. Lakhan and Sagan feel a vague sense of loyalty to him. Lakhan hopes to get his sister married off to Birsa sometime next year, if possible. What can he do? After a brief dilemma, Lakhan follows Birsa. Sagan, the youngest of the three, looks hopelessly confused. But he always does what the other two do. So he, too, turns away, leaving Arif, Narasingh, and Raimoti standing at the junction.

The three shapes recede into the enveloping darkness and fade away. Raimoti pulls a dirty rag from his pocket and gently wipes the blood off Arif's face. Narasingh, the youngest of them all—he is barely seventeen—is visibly shaken. His face is ashen, and his eyes are open wide with fear. There is a fine sheen of perspiration on his brow. "What do we do now, *kaka*? We are all alone."

Raimoti laughs. "Alone? Are we now? I would never have guessed. Don't you know, son, that it is human destiny to be alone? Every life is a long, lonely journey. Ha ha! But I guess you are too young to realize that. Anyway, we better hurry. Within minutes, this place will start flooding, too. How do you feel, Arif? Can you walk?"

"Uh, yes," Arif replies with a groan. "The motherfucker really kicked my guts out. Let me catch him back on the surface, that son of a tattered cunt!"

"Later, later. Come, put on your helmet and let's move! And you really have a foul tongue in your mouth. Rascal!"

Raimoti turns right and walks briskly into the tunnel. They can hear the sound of water gushing from behind them quite distinctly. Raimoti wonders how long Birsa and his friends will last, but only briefly. He has more pressing things on his mind. He is calculating how long it will be before water from the fresh breach reaches them. He reckons they have to walk about one and a half kilometers to reach the skip landing. They are not moving fast enough. Water flows faster. About halfway down, he remembers there is a dip in the seam—a kind of trough, almost half a kilometer long. He must cross that before the water hits them. The trough will win them a few precious minutes. But if they are caught while still in that depression, they will surely be swamped and drowned. Not a very pleasant thought.

Sages, saints, gods—they have all tried to explain the fragility of life. They have talked of the destructibility of the body and the permanence of the soul. They have taught how one must rise above the mundaneness of existence and apply one's mind to higher truths and dive deeper into knowledge. Few of those saints have ever been trapped in an underground coal mine that is flooding. If any did, probably none survived to give their homilies.

Down here, Raimoti creates his own little philosophies—minuscule processes of thoughts, compared to the Vedas, but enlightening in their own ways: keep the breeze in your face—it leads to the skip shaft; keep the sound of water as far behind as you can—it prevents drowning; don't run—you might fall and sprain a foot; don't walk too slow—you might never make it past the trough; don't think—it might paralyze you . . .

He marvels at the convoluted workings of the Almighty, who made man the crown of His creations and yet made him so fragile and inept. Man cannot swim like fish, can't fly like birds, can't run like deer, can't jump like monkeys, can't see like owls, cannot even think like any of them. A pity. Yet the desire to live burns so strong. Man's life is an eggshell, with the elephant of circumstances always hovering just inches away. Who knows when the elephant decides to step on the egg?

But too many thoughts of eggs and elephants in a coal mine is distracting. So Raimoti trots on till they are quite out of breath. He stops for a moment. He can hear the panting of his mates following him but doesn't have the strength to speak. Suddenly, there is a sharp rustling behind—the Beast has caught up with them!

Raimoti feels its slobbering tongue around his feet. He recoils in horror and looks down. A thin, cool film of water is rushing past him, becoming thicker every moment. He can hear the hungry panting behind him clearly. It is so near.

"*Kaka!*" Narasingh whimpers. "What do we do now? Water has reached us!"

"Don't panic, boy! Let me think."

"Think fast, *kaka*—else we will all drown!"

"Wait!"

Ahead is the skip shaft, still a mile away. But the dip in the mine seam is closer.

Oh! Water is rising so fast—look! It is almost covering my ankles now. We will never make it. Why can't we men fly, Lord? Or swim? Or just lie down and die? Wait . . . there was a connection to Mine Number 2 somewhere on this level. It was close to the dip, to the east. Wait!

"Arif?" Raimoti asks excitedly. "Do you remember the last

phase of Mine Number Two? Where you and I worked the south-
ern tip?"

"*Kaka*," Arif replies wearily, "I remember. But let me remind
you that we are in Mine Number Three, not Two."

"I know, I know. But do you remember how we were asked to
repair some stoppage and you protested?"

"Yes, I didn't think it was our job. Repairs were to be done by
a different gang. But what the hell is your point, old man?"

"My point is that finally, the supervisor forced you to work
on that stoppage, and later, you told me how you cheated him and
didn't make the barrier as thick as you were instructed to. In fact,
you told me that the barrier was barely two bricks thick in many
places. How we laughed, remember?"

"Of course I do. Making a fortress in that dead end made no
sense. The bastard just wanted to give me some extra work as a
punishment. But what of it?" Arif asks impatiently.

"I later found out why the supervisor was so insistent. That
was an important job. It was an opening to a narrow connection
between Number Two and Three! The supervisor told me later
that before the existing entrance to this mine was opened, the engineers made a short, narrow tunnel connecting the two coal seams,
in order to explore and analyze samples. Later, they decided on a
new entrance site. They sealed the connecting shaft but did not
stow it with sand. That wall that you were asked to repair was the
only barrier between the two mines. The other end opens into a
small hall on this side."

"Great! So we know that Mines Number Two and Three are
connected somewhere. And how does that help us? Look, *kaka,*

while you tell us these interesting bits of local mining history, water is rising around us. It's almost knee-deep now. Let's run ahead from here on, one last dash to the skip landing."

"Arif, I also know that there was a short gully from the hall, connecting to this corridor somewhere very close to the dip that lies ahead. We have never worked in this section, so you wouldn't know. But I have seen that hall once when the assistant engineer *sahib* called me there to ask something. I remember the gully because it looked a little odd compared to the other corridors that cross this main passage."

"*Kaka,* I think you might have something there, but how will you differentiate that particular gully from all these dozens of cross-corridors branching out of this passage?"

"I remember that it was along the northern wall, and it sloped down, while all others sloped up or were level. I think I can recognize it if I see it."

"Slope *down*?" Arif says incredulously. "If it slopes *down,* it is the last place we should enter, *kaka*. It will be the first place to get flooded. Why don't we hit the skip landing, as planned?"

"Because, Arif, we won't make it. We will have chest-deep water here in under ten minutes, and we would be entering the dip portion about then. By the time we cross it, water would be far above our heads. Do you swim? Or does Narasingh? I don't." The two shake their heads despondently. Neither knows how to swim. "So," Raimoti continues with greater conviction, "the only solution lies in trying out our luck in that connecting shaft. Once we reach the hall, we will find the exit. I am sure we can break down the flimsy barrier you repaired in no time with our crowbars. We will be out of this mine, and the exit door of Mine Number Two isn't far from there."

"B-but," Narasingh interjects timidly for the first time, "what if this side of the shaft is sealed more strongly? We will be caught in the hall, won't we? Or what if the gully leading to the hall is sealed off?"

"Almighty be praised! The boy is right, *kaka*. What if that happens?" Arif asks.

"Then we die—or think of something else. But I really believe our best chance lies in that shaft. Are you with me or are you not?"

Arif and Narasingh look at each other, doubt written large on their faces. The choice is not easy. They know that the skip landing is their safest escape route. At the same time, they realize that the threat of being overtaken by the deluge en route is quite real. Neither of them is as experienced or intuitive about underground mines as Raimoti. At this stage, they do not want to break away from him. He seems so sure of himself—perhaps he is right.

"Fine, *kaka*," Arif finally says with a sigh, "you lead us on. Now that we have trusted our souls to the devil, we might as well trust our bodies to you! Ha, ha, ha! Lead on, you madman!"

Quickly, Raimoti turns and sprints away with amazing speed and agility, splashing through the churningblack water. Even as they run, they can feel the water level rise till it is almost waist-high. They pass several cross-tunnels, but Raimoti presses on. Suddenly, he stops at a relatively narrow opening to their left. The opening is raised, so there is only a thin layer of water cascading down the slightly sloped floor. Without any hesitation, Raimoti jumps up the threshold and jogs down, Arif and Narasingh following in a daze. It feels like running on a river—talk of saints walking on water! Black spray flies in all directions as they hurtle downward. In a few seconds, the floor levels out, and the narrow gully broadens to become a roughly oval hall, about five meters high, twenty meters wide, and thirty meters long. There is about two feet of water here, but the area is filling up fast. One end of the hall slopes up sharply and ends in a sort of narrow ledge. Behind the ledge, close to the ceiling, is a patch of wall that looks different from the rest of the black surface: it is the sealed exit to the connecting shaft.

"Oh my God! *Kaka!* This exit is sealed—like Shaitan's arse! Oh God! What shall we do now, *kaka*? We are trapped!" Arif moans.

Raimoti is silent. There is nothing to say. Returning to the main corridor is pointless—they have lost too much time in coming here and now will have to run against the flow of water up a slope. It is quite useless. They have to do something here and do it quickly.

Raimoti clambers up the rough surface to the narrow ledge. The foothold is precarious—not a good surface on which to stand and make an attempt to break down the barrier. Raimoti hammers the sealed exit with his crowbar. There is only a dull, hollow sound, and a few pieces of brick and mortar crumble and splash into the water below. It looks quite sturdy. Without a word, both Arif and Narasingh understand their grim situation. There is no alternative left—they need to try to break down the barrier. They climb up the steep slope and join Raimoti in a frenzied battering of the sealed exit. Minutes pass, and water rises like boilingblack milk in a cauldron. On the floor of the hall, the level of water has risen to almost shoulder-height.

On the narrow, slippery ledge, the three miners are relentless in their hammering. Chunks of the wall start to fall off, but someone has done a much better job of sealing the shaft on this side than Arif did at the other end. They still can't break through. They are out of breath.

Raimoti climbs down to check the water level. It is up to his chin. He climbs back to the ledge.

He turns toward the gully entrance where all the water is cascading in and sees the gaping jaws of the Beast. Its mouth is open wide in cruel glee, and Raimoti can see the black fangs trickling a stickyblack fluid. It makes his stomach churn. The Beast opens its jaws wider to encompass the entire hall in its vapid depths. Raimoti ducks in fright and smashes his crowbar into the nearest tooth. It is huge and glistens with the black blood of generations of miners. The roar is deafening. Raimoti strikes hard and then strikes again. The massive tooth breaks loose and falls like a ton of coal. Before his horrified eyes, the jagged tooth turns slowly in midair and impales a frozen Narasingh in the head.

There is a soft, ominous sound. The sound has a certain sickening finality about it, like an elephant standing on an eggshell. For a second Narasingh seems to sprout a triangular black head of coal. Then he teeters on the ledge, blood spouting out of his nose, eyes, mouth, and ears. He stretches a slim arm toward Raimoti and falls into the black void below. Even amid the thundering sound of water, that splash reverberates through Raimoti's soul like an underground blast. Arif is motionless. Raimoti turns his headlamp down toward the water.

There! There is the lad. How calm and relaxed a smashed egg can look. Or a coconut. In fact, the peacefulness of his face is more of a coconut cracked open in a temple: a thin, clean fissure with sweet, clear liquid oozing out slowly. Only the liquid oozing out from his head is not clear—it is red, bloodred, and Raimoti is certain it isn't sweet, either. It is salty, like tears.

They watch the strange sight, mesmerized by its ghastliness. Water still rises below them, but it is perceptibly slower. The hunger of the Beast has subsided—at least for the moment—and he has left them in relative peace to gorge himself on his latest prey. Narasingh's head floats on the dark water like a coconut smeared red with vermilion and offered to the gods. All at once the ledge trembles and, with a subdued crack, crumbles in two. Arif's portion tumbles into the water, and he falls with it. Raimoti has a tiny patch of the ledge still remaining under his feet. He peers down to find Arif thrashing about in the water, going under every now and then.

Raimoti slides down to sit on the ledge, scrawny legs dangling over the water. He extends his crowbar to Arif, who grabs it with a desperation that only a drowning man can possess. Raimoti pulls slowly, inch by slimy inch, till Arif is within arm's reach. Arif is sputtering and coughing out water but is otherwise uninjured. Water has almost reached the ledge, and Raimoti has no difficulty pulling Arif close to his knees. He observes with a detached feeling that the water level has stopped rising. Perhaps they are caught in an air pocket.

There isn't enough space on what was left of the ledge to allow both of them to sit. Arif is happy just dangling from Raimoti's knees, immersed in liquid coal up to his shoulders. With only a moment's reluctance, Raimoti throws away the crowbar and grips Arif's shivering hands in his. He won't need the crowbar anymore. They hang on the precipice with little black waves lapping at them like puppies, making wet, squelching noises.

chapter 5

Water trickles down the sides of Bibhash's mouth and forms a worrydark ring around his collar as he takes a nervous swallow. Bibhash feels like throwing up. *This is it,* he thinks miserably, *it's all going to come down on me.* He notices the tremble in his hands and quickly hides them under the table. As the subarea manager, he has to react immediately, assess the gravity of the situation, and launch a rescue mission. The inquisition, the witch-hunting, the blame shoveling will come later. For the moment he has to deal with the inevitable mob before they lynch him. This is the nightmare for every manager. *Why me? Why, Kariakhani?* he asks of the heavens. *Why the fuck me?*

He realizes that even now irate laborers will be assembling at the pit head, screaming for the blood of the management. He will have to get past the barricade of their mindless wrath before a rescue operation can start. Horror stories from colleagues and seniors who were trapped in such situations explode like firecrackers in his head. Mr. Sahay, he recalls, was the assistant manager when the Barner roof fall occurred. Three hundred men slapped him, breaking his jaw. A lover of nonvegetarian food, Mr. Sahay has remained a chaste vegetarian ever since because he cannot chew anything tough. It's been five years now. And Das *da*? After the Joonidih disaster, he went completely mad. The spontaneous gas and coal-dust explosion killed two miners and blinded one. Das *da* rushed underground, leading the paramedics and disappearing for several hours. He was found the next morning in an alley in the *dhowrah* settlement with third-degree burns over 75 percent of his body. Das *da* was in a coma for six weeks, and when he revived, he refused to wear clothes. Even after a lapse of eleven years and despite a prolonged treatment organized by his family, Das *da* can spring from his office chair and tear off all his clothes before pouring glasses of water down his burn-wrinkled skin to quell the "heat of flames."

Bibhash shudders at these horrid recollections of what a mob of panic-stricken and infuriated laborers can do to a manager, whom they consider their first enemy—a symbol of all the factors responsible for their miseries. And who can blame them, really? The heat, the dust, the ear-piercing shriek of drills, the paranatural ambience of the underground, and the perpetual dread of the unpredictable—these are causes enough for their collective emotional and mental instability.

These mines are incubators for spawns of the devil. They breed dark thoughts, nurture anger, and spit out men—more creatures than men, more bestial than creatures—of suppressed violence. *What dreadful power causes this? What twisted hands—what squirming brain? With what angry intent?* Bibhash wonders hysterically, his mind fast losing its grip on reality. Metaphysical questions of some dead poet flit around randomly in his head like burning fireflies. *Who is the Beast that forges such things?*

"Bibhash!" The angry bellow from Pandey*ji* plucks him out of a metaphysical abyss. "*Arre,* what are you gaping at? Go out with these workers and find out what's happening while Karna *sahib* and I finish our dinner. One can never trust what they say— these *ganwars.* Damn fools."

"But *sahib,*" Ram Babu tries to interject, "I was there when it happened. Workers are running out of the mine, and water is flooding in so fast that we fear Level Two has been half submerged and water has reached the belt conveyor. Some of the ventilation ducts also seem to have choked up."

"*Dhat!* Are you an engineer? You people start panicking like a bunch of village women at the first sign of danger. Bibhash! What are you waiting for, a *palki*? Go and inspect and report back to us in half an hour. Sorry, Karna *sahib, saar.* Want some more *biryani,* please?"

With a heavy and unsteady tread, Bibhash follows the group of workers out as they all pile into his jeep. Whiskey and fear are a deadly mix for fast driving, and the men cling to the rattling frame for support as Bibhash hurtles down the darkwinding road to the pit head. There is already a considerable crowd of men coagulated around the towering headgear of the winder, the mechanism that pulls up the cage or skip. The whole area is awash in sodium-vapor floodlights, adding an eerieorange tint to everything, like a scene from the *Inferno.* There are alarms and sirens clanging and hooting from everywhere, and dozens of people are scampering about looking completely lost and confused. Someone has managed to switch on the emergency pump sets, and a pipe has burst somewhere, spraying everything with cold water and transforming the surrounding ground into a pool of slushy black mud.

Bibhash slams on the brakes, and the jeep skids to an abrupt halt just outside the fenced enclosure to the mine entrance. He tries to jump off, as an active subarea manager is supposed to, but slips and falls painfully on the muddy ground. No one comes to his aid. The men who accompanied him have gravitated like iron filings to the magnet of the winder. Bibhash gets up with some difficulty and tries to enter the barrier of jostling miners. He is at the periphery of the crowd, and his mud-stained clothes allow him to merge with it. So far no one seems to be bothered by his presence.

"What happened?" he asks of the man standing ahead of him.

"It's that lake," the man shouts back over the din of a hundred people screaming. "Arif's gang was working on Level Two, cutting into the barrier of water. We think they could have cut too deep, or possibly there was an underground extension of the lake that they tapped into. But all of a sudden there was an explosion, like a cloudburst, and water gushed in from the lake. The gangs working below in Level One heard it and realized that there was a breach. They managed to run to Connection Number Five, where the old stopping has crumbled. By the time they climbed up, there was a river flowing down from the lake. Somehow they reached the Level Two skip landing. They sounded the alarm, and the skip was raised just before the landing got flooded."

"But," Bibhash asks breathlessly, "there were two other gangs working in the syncline part of Level Two itself—what about them?"

"Oh! They were quite close to the adit connecting to the Level One cage landing. They managed to escape without even getting wet. The gods must be with them."

"How many inside?" Bibhash asks.

But the man has lost interest in him and is pushing to get closer to the shaft. Bibhash follows in his wake and reaches the main landing, where Balwant, the gigantic mining *sirdar*—a supervisor—is directing a dozen men trying to form a sort of rescue chain. After a great deal of maneuvering and elbowing, Bibhash reaches close enough to shout to Balwant. "*Ai! Ai!* Balwant! *Oye!* Balwant!"

The mining *sirdar* looks up and peers into the crowd pressing in to him from all sides. He doesn't recognize his subarea manager in the melee.

"*Haat bahin-chod!* Move back—get away from the landing. I only need strong men around here. *Peechche—peechche!* God knows where that prick Mukherjee is. *Oye!* Ram Singh, lash out with your cane at anyone who tries to step onto the landing."

"Balwant!" Bibhash screams desperately, evading the swishing cane of Ram Singh. "It's me—Mukherjee! Let me get in."

Balwant peers suspiciously at the bedraggled little man before him, then a glimmer of recognition dawns on his pinched face. "*Oye! Sirji*, you? Come, come. *Oye! Saale* Ram Singh, let *sahib* come in."

Ram Singh swiftly turns his vicious swishing elsewhere, valiantly hammering the unstoppable crowd of workers away from the landing like Horatio.

"What happened here?" Bibhash inquires.

Balwant relates the information in more or less the same sequence as the earlier man.

"When did this happen?"

"About forty minutes back. There is Ram Babu! *Oye!* Ram Babu, come and tell *sahib*—sir*ji,* he was there below, on Level Two, when it happened."

Ram Babu steps out of the crowd, ducking below the continuous swish of Ram Singh's cane. "*Sahib,* I was with Lalji's gang in Level Two when we heard the loud crash from the lakeside. I immediately suspected that it was a water burst. I ordered the gang to evacuate and pressed the alarm switch. There were two other gangs working on that level: one farther down, to the west, and the other on the extreme east end, where the breach took place. We ran down the slope of the syncline, along the belt conveyor. By the time we reached the adit, we could see water flooding the washout trough. So I retreated west, but the noise of the water was so great that I realized there would probably be too little time to reach the skip landing for Level Two, from where we could have climbed to safety. So we returned to the adit and crawled up the second ventilator incline and got near the Level Three cage landing. Luckily, Bhola, who was leading the second gang on Level Two syncline, thought of the same plan, and we managed to escape in the nick of time."

"And what about the gangs on Level One?" Bibhash asks,

trying to think clearly about the layout of the intricate multi-tiered maze underground.

"*Sahib*," Ram Babu says with awe, "they are surely the luckiest miners alive. When I left for the guesthouse to inform you, they were still trapped below. Buddha Deb was down there with four other gangs. When he heard the water burst, his people simply panicked. They were in much greater danger, being on the lowest level. Buddha Deb realized that even if they reached Level Two, they might be swept away by the force of water. But he also realized that if they delayed their attempt, Level One was certain to get completely flooded within minutes. So he bullied the four gangs into taking the calculated risk of striking for the Level Two skip landing. He led them to the old connection between Level One and Level Two, where he remembered that the stopping, or stone barrier, had broken down. They emerged about half a kilometer to the east of the skip landing. That was when the lighting short-circuited and the corridor was plunged into darkness. As they ran down toward the skip landing, the flood overtook them. But Buddha Deb coaxed the men to keep running, till they reached the landing. They entered the washout-trough area and practically swam across three hundred meters to the higher side and made a dash for the skip landing. All twenty-six of them managed to escape even before the trough was totally submerged. That, *sahib*, is a miracle if ever there was one."

"Total, how many down in this pit tonight?" Bibhash asks.

"Twenty-six on Level One and twenty-two on Level Two, *sahib*."

"How many have come out?"

"Forty-two, *sahib*."

"Who is left?"

"Just Arif's gang: Birsa, Sagan, Lakhan, Narasingh, Raimoti, and Arif."

"Any chance they may have survived?"

"Sir*ji*," Balwant butts in, "I don't think so—judging by the reports. But I thought we should send a team down to Level Three and, if possible, to Level Two to check just how bad things are. To start with, these four men from the rescue room are going down the skip to Level Three—that is, sir*ji*, if we have your permission. The cage might be too risky under the circumstances."

"Yes, of course, do that. In the meantime, I will rush to the guesthouse and inform the GM *sahib* and call up our own CGM *sahib*. Has anyone informed the police and fire brigade?"

"Sir*ji*," Balwant replies, "I called up the police *thana*, but they said that the *daroga sahib* is out of town. The subinspector in charge is new and is trying to raise the deputy superintendent of police on the wireless to seek guidance. He says that mine accidents are not law-and-order situations and that he is understaffed for patrolling tonight, as it is, so he refuses to send a team here without first clearing it with the DSP."

"I—I will try to talk to him. What about the fire brigade?"

"Sir*ji*, I think their phone is out of order. It is coming in continuously busy. I have sent a rider on a motorbike to fetch them, but it might take some time, since the fire station is at least forty-five kilometers away."

"Good, good," Bibhash says with relief. At least someone has taken the basic precautions after the accident. It will read well on the report that he will send to headquarters. Balwant, he concludes warmly, is a solid chap. "So you carry on with the rescue operation while I try to get in touch with the CGM *sahib*."

As Balwant and his rescue team prepare to descend into the mine shaft, Bibhash quietly sidles away from the landing platform. The crowd is reluctant to let him leave. There are grim murmurs about the fault of the management in the accident, about the lack of responsiveness. Bibhash is feeling suffocated. Mob control is not what they taught at the Institute of Mining. And where the hell is the surveyor? If he could lay his hands on the fellow, he would throw him to the lions in this arena. All he wants to do for the moment is to leave this place and lock himself up in his room in the guesthouse. He will go back, fall sick, and let that pompous arsehole Pandey*ji* tackle it. It wouldn't be too far from the truth— Bibhash really is feeling sick with anxiety. He remembers that he hadn't read the surveyor's report that morning, what with the sudden news of the VIP's arrival. What if it contained a hidden warning of impending disaster? He doesn't even want to think about it now. He sidles through the restive crowd, vaguely promising to return with GM *sahib* soon.

He clambers into his aged jeep and cranks the ignition several times before the wretched machine splutters to life. He floors the accelerator pedal and skids out of the compound, slewing dangerously through the muck, scattering the crowd about him. Six miners feared dead. Oh God! How is he ever going to deal with the mess? He knows that for him, things can only get worse. The aftermath will bring its inquiry, and everyone will be looking for a scapegoat. Who better than Bibhash, the subarea manager, to pin all the guilt on? But has he done anything wrong? Has he been negligent? Bibhash is not too sure.

It isn't as if he is the most diligent of managers around, but he is certainly not careless. He is too scared to be careless. He likes sticking to the book of rules; it is safer. At least he can always claim having followed prescribed procedures if things go wrong. He has staunchly avoided making any big decisions through his career. Decisions lay one open to personalized criticism, and Bibhash cannot cope with the trauma of being publicly dissected by strangers. Some say he lacks initiative, that he lacks the drive to reach the top. That is just fine by him. He doesn't want to reach the top. He will feel too exposed, too insecure, up there. Is there ever any peace in climbing up the unending ladder? His attitude toward his work and his inherent insecurity have not made him popular with his superiors. His subordinates are indifferent, at best, to his deliberate lack of leadership. So Bibhash doesn't see any of them coming to his rescue if he is burned at the stake. This realization churns his innards into an acidic pulp. He breaks to a halt on an empty stretch, leans over, and throws up his dinner. It doesn't make him feel any better.

He thinks of Sunita, his wife of twelve years, back in the city. She teaches in a company-aided school and looks after their two children, Swati and Supriya. Sunita is a good wife and an excellent mother, but there is no love between her and Bibhash. Whatever little affection they had for each other in the first couple of years of married life has evaporated steadily under the scorching heat of insufficient income and forced separation. Bibhash has spent barely four years posted in the same town as Sunita, and even that total has been spread over slots of one or two years at a stretch. He can hardly blame Sunita when she complains that he has never been around when she really needed him. Bibhash remembers the time when Sunita's belly was swollen with Swati. They had been married for two years, and their bad feelings had not started to fester yet. They were both happy about the new development in their dreary lives. But when Sunita was in her second trimester, the company had posted Bibhash to the Phaguni area, where the nearest hospital took three torturous hours to reach on a bumpy country road. Bibhash had tried hard to get his transfer canceled or even postponed by a few months, but he had no godfather to back him. So in the sixth month of Sunita's pregnancy, he had to leave her. The company, in its munificence, promised him a month's leave around the time of the delivery. Sunita cried and cried till her tears ran dry and her blood pressure shot up.

Bibhash called her parents and pleaded with them to come down for a few months to take care of Sunita. Sunita's father, a successful lawyer in Vishnupur, disdainfully agreed to send his wife down till Bibhash managed to get leave. He sincerely felt he had committed a grave mistake in marrying his daughter to a mining engineer. Sunita's mother did not have a high opinion of her son-in-law, either. She was always complaining about how little Bibhash earned and how he was incapable of running his house without their financial support. Sunita was a pretty, convent-educated girl, and her mother felt they could have gotten her a much better match, had it not been for the fact that Bibhash's father was an old friend from Calcutta. Often she made oblique suggestions that if

Bibhash found his income insufficient, he could easily supplement it with "a little extra" under the table. That made him furious. Not because he had never thought of it but because he knew he would never have the courage to accept bribes. His inability to emulate what many of his colleagues had been doing for years without the slightest bit of trouble made him feel deficient and impotent. It was not a matter of ethics—it was a matter of guts. And he hated it when his mother-in-law criticized him for it. He'd had roaring arguments with her over this till Sunita had threatened suicide if the two didn't lay off. That was when she decided that as soon as she could, she would take a job to add to their income.

Sunita developed some serious complications with her placenta, and her parents whisked her off to Vishnupur for the last two months of her confinement, without informing Bibhash. When he found out, Bibhash felt hurt and helpless and drank himself to oblivion in Phaguni. He didn't go for the delivery and visited his wife and newborn daughter only after three weeks. Sunita stayed with her parents for another year while Bibhash moved the heavens in his efforts to get posted back to his headquarters. Finally, someone took pity on him, and he returned to the town and got Sunita back. As soon as Swati was two, Sunita picked up a job as a teacher in a company-aided school. They had a relatively stable life for a year and a half, when the company decided that Bibhash had enjoyed enough of their indulgence, and he was posted to an exploration site where there were leaking tents in the name of accommodation. Sunita stayed behind in the three-room company-provided quarters.

The birth of their second daughter, Supriya, was very nearly an action replay of their first experience. But by then Sunita had learned to expect the worst. She had made arrangements for her sister and mother to each spend a few months with her. Once again she went to Vishnupur for her delivery and spent a year there. By the time she resumed her job, the company had opened a well-equipped day-care center where she could drop off her children while she went to work. The next time Bibhash managed a posting back to the town, he noticed that Sunita had changed in an imperceptible but drastic way. She had become withdrawn, indifferent, and cocooned. There was nothing he could put his finger on; it was just that she had distanced herself from him. She cooked dishes he liked, she took care of the children, she went to official parties and functions with him, she even allowed him to have sex with her. But it was as if there were two Sunitas: one whom she shared with Bibhash and the other whom she kept locked up within her—unreachable, untouchable. She no longer reacted to her husband's absence or lack of involvement in her daily existence. There were no more tantrums, no more tears, just polite apathy. Bibhash could do nothing to change it.

Sometimes, in remote exploration camps or transit rooms, he would sit with photo albums of his wife and children and spend hours poring over the photographs he had taken on his infrequent visits home.

Home—that is also a strange word in his life. Despite having one, and despite having a family, he has no place he can truly consider his home. For months on end, the only home he has is a crumblyellow room of a field guesthouse in some mining area, with only flies and mosquitoes for company in the evenings. He is a voracious reader, especially of the classics and nineteenth-century English poets, and his books sustain him through these prolonged spells of intellectual isolation. He goes to work, follows laid-down procedures, and returns, his days blending seamlessly into one another. He does what he has to do without enthusiasm, without dislike, without a desire to succeed. It's merely something to fill up the murky hollow of time.

Why is he doing it? For whom? He often asks himself, as he sits alone in the evenings, finishing his daily nip of rum, eating his favorite snack of boiled lotus stems and peanuts and listening to Pink Floyd and mournful *ghazals: music that moistens the parched spirit like soft dew on the petals of burnt roses*. Every night, as he drinks himself to sleep, praying to an uncaring divinity: *Give me dreamful ease or comforting darkness or death.*

Bibhash swerves the jeep into the semicircular drive and stops by the porch. The housekeeping staff is standing on the veranda, talking in hushed tones. He can hear music wafting from the lobby, where, presumably, the VIP guests are enjoying an after-dinner show on the TV.

"Sahib," the cook steps forward and asks, "what is the situation at the mine?"

"Things are fine. We are pumping out the water, and the police have been informed. Now step aside—I've got to report to GM *sahib* and then make some phone calls. Go and put some ice and lemons in my room."

Bibhash brushes past the men and enters the lobby. Pandey*ji* and Karna *sahib* are sitting in front of the TV, watching the popular show *Antakshari*. Pandey*ji* tears his eyes away from the screen and looks disinterestedly at Bibhash. "*Han!* You're back? What took you so long?" he asks indignantly, as if he has been anxiously waiting for news instead of watching *Antakshari.* "And what have you done to your clothes? You look filthy and stink like dung!"

"Sorry, sir, but I slipped in mud at the pit head. The . . . the situation is quite bad out there. Levels One and Two seem to have flooded completely, and water is filling up fast on Level Three. Out of the forty-eight workers inside, forty-two have been successfully evacuated. Six are still trapped inside, and we fear they might have drowned."

This has the expected effect of shaking Pandey*ji* from his in-souciance. "What? Six feared dead? Have the police been informed? And the fire brigade? Why haven't you ordered a rescue operation? We should at least make an attempt, I feel."

Pandey*ji* is sounding crisp and efficient. It is for the benefit of Karna *sahib,* who is still quite engrossed in the TV show. Pandey*ji* is comfortable in the awareness that whatever happens, he is not involved. But that doesn't mean he will not hog the limelight and the credit of mounting a rescue operation. Only he doesn't know what Bibhash has in store for him.

"Sir, I think there is a potential labor unrest situation taking shape out there. It is indeed providential that we have the GM of personnel with us today. You are the perfect person to handle the men there. I have to make some calls to headquarters and also try to speak to the local police and administration. I think it will be extremely advantageous if you go down to the mine and talk to the workers. They will be happy to find senior management so respon-sive, sir—you know how popular you are with the workers."

Pandey*ji* is torn between the desire to project himself as a man of action, leading from the front, and the apprehension of being caught up in a possible riot. If he goes now, he might be able to avert an ugly turn of events, and that will be a big trumpet in his hands to blow in the ears of his superiors. But if, on the other hand, things get out of control and the workers go on a rampage, he could jeopardize his till now unblemished record as a personnel manager. As a consequence of these astute ponderings, the balance tilts in favor of caution. So without sounding fazed, Pandey*ji* tells Bibhash that he would rather wait till Bibhash can speak to the authorities and then accompany him to the mine. In the meantime, Pandey*ji* asks Bibhash to brief him fully on the accident and then go and change into something less malodorous. When Bibhash leaves for his room, Pandey*ji* turns his attention to Karna *sahib*, who has switched off the TV and is looking quite anxious.

"So sorry, so sorry, *saar*," Pandey*ji* says, "but one has to get involved, you see. Even though all this is not really my headache, a man in my position must provide guidance and leadership to these field engineers—they can be so unfocused in such situations, you know."

Karna *sahib* says, "Quite, quite. I'm quite impressed by the way you've—ah—handled things. Could you give me a—umm—self-contained note on this whole damn thing by morning? Eh? Have to call up and brief my superiors first thing tomorrow morning. The ministry must know the details, and it is fortunate that I am here, on site, so to speak."

"Sure, *saar*. Sure, *saar*," Pandey*ji* says happily. He is great at self-contained notes, especially when the draft will be prepared by

Bibhash. He intends to command the subarea manager to write out a draft before leaving for the mine, then append his signature and claim the credit. "You shall have it in the morning, *saar.*"

"Good, good." Karna *sahib* looks relieved. He will have a nice background note for his early-morning reportage to his bosses, before the press gets involved. That should impress people. "In that case, is there anything I can do here? I'm sure you are—ah—quite capable of handling the—ummm—situation—I intend to make a mention of it to the higher-ups."

"No, *saar*—no, *saar*, please," Pandey*ji* whines in delight. "You must rest, *saar*. These things are routine for us miners. Part of the job hazard. You've had a long, tiring day, *saar*. You must rest now—don't worry, *saar*, I'm here to take care of things, *saar*."

"Yes, yes, in that case, I guess I will—ah—call it a day and—umm—hit the bed now, leaving you chaps to do your rescue stuff and all that—eh?"

"Absolutely, absolutely, *saar*. The AC has been on since dinner, *saar*. I wish you good night, *saar*. Unfortunately, we managers must continue through the night. Good night, *saar*."

"Good night," Karna *sahib* says with a huge yawn, getting up to leave. "Oh! By the way, Mr. Pandey, I hope there is a mosquito repellent in the room. There are too many mosquitoes in this damned place."

"*Saar*, I will send someone to attend to you. Good night, *saar*."

While Pandey*ji* and Karna *sahib* are engaged in all this serious business, Bibhash prepares to take a shower in his room. He has managed to get through to the deputy superintendent of police, who has promised to pass the message down to the *thana* or to send a contingent over to the mine. He also assured Bibhash that they will get in touch with the fire brigade and someone will be there within the next hour or so. Bibhash doesn't want to return to the pit head before the authorities are there—he doesn't want to face the crowd without police protection. He has also spoken with the wife of his chief general manager, who has informed him that Mishra *sahib* is out at dinner and that she will ask him to call back as soon as he returns, which should be within the next hour or so. There is nothing to do in the meantime, so Bibhash has a quick shot of rum with lemon and takes a shower. Usually, he doesn't drink after dinner—most nights he is already too drunk by then—but today is different. After having thrown up earlier, he is feeling much lighter, and he needs something to keep him going through this ordeal.

He washes and changes into clean clothes, dabbing on a generous measure of cheap cologne to reduce the stink, producing a heady aura of alcohol and minty fragrance around him. He sits down to write the two-pager on the accident that Pandey*ji* has asked him to submit before morning. Bibhash enjoys writing and does a good job of it, using short, crisp sentences to bring out the most crucial developments and details. He cannot avoid the temptation of highlighting his prompt inspection of the site and his efforts to contact civil authorities. The report is ready in under half an hour, and Bibhash locks his door and stretches out on his bed for a much needed breather.

He pours out another stiff measure of rum from the bottle at his bedside and adds several cubes of ice. He is feeling much better.

He is calmer, and his perception has turned less cloudy. He feels relaxed—for the moment, at least. On impulse, he pulls out a *Hustler* that he keeps hidden under his mattress. He flips through the thick magazine, pausing for a few seconds on each page, admiring the unabashed display of feminine charms. In moments of great depression, he finds pornography a good distraction—it is rather uplifting, in more than one way.

Sunita is pretty in her own way. Bibhash used to enjoy having sex with her in the initial years of their marriage. But over the past few years, especially since the birth of their second daughter, he finds sex with his wife a traumatic experience. Not that Sunita ever denies him his conjugal rights—it's just that she is so uninvolved. Months of separation leave Bibhash in a turgid state of anxiety whenever he visits his family. Sunita is conscious of this fact and even appears understanding about his eagerness to sleep with her. So she lies down in the bed next to him and offers no resistance to his frenzied exploration of her body till, finally, Bibhash climbs atop her and spends himself in a few seconds. Without a word, she takes a shower, then drinks some water and turns away to sleep soundly, while Bibhash stays up the rest of the night, manhandling subsequent outbursts of desire. He never has the courage to be more demanding and feels grateful for the allowances his wife makes. He continues having statutory sex with Sunita more out of a sense of propriety than out of arousal. It is almost as if he is scared to let this last strand of togetherness between them break, setting them adrift in their separate oceans of unhappiness. But this strand is growing weaker and thinner by the day.

Bibhash is not one to take his love to town, into the domain of professionals. He is a very private man and has discovered a private remedy: pornography. Gradually, he has pieced together an enviable collection of erotic literature, photographs, and videos that act as life buoys in his lonely ocean. Surprisingly, he has started enjoying making love to himself more than he enjoys making love to his wife. At least his hands don't rush off to take a shower, and they don't fall asleep after he has ejaculated. His hands don't scare him, either. So while he turns the well-thumbed pages of *Hustler* and waits for Pandey*ji* to call him, Bibhash decides to have another go at it. It is difficult to turn the pages and jerk off simultaneously, but he manages to bring himself to a satisfying climax and lies there spent and exhausted. He pours himself another glass of rum and settles down to unsettling thoughts.

In this ocean of life, I displace no water, Bibhash thinks dejectedly, wiping his palm on the bedsheet. His parents have both been dead for years, and he is an only child. His children are practically strangers and, like their mother, feel that he is not a part of their lives. He has no one he can call a friend. His subordinates don't respect him, his colleagues are indifferent, and his superiors don't even think about him. In short, he feels, he is a rather unnecessary intrusion on the world. He feels like one of those cheap papier-mâché *kathakali* masks that hang on the drawing room walls in the homes of lower-middle-class families, without contributing to the decor or detracting from the squalor. Each just hangs—hangs and gathers dust and cobwebs—slowly losing shine and color, becoming another brick in the wall.

He hears a sudden commotion from outside and quickly finishes his drink. He hurriedly zips up his fly and sits up unsteadily, taking a while to find his balance. Someone is pounding on his door feverishly. He gargles from the water bottle, spits into the plastic wastepaper basket next to his bed, and opens the door.

It's the *durbaan.* "*Sahib,* there are some workers from the mine. They—they are very angry and demanding to know what you are doing here. They have *gheraoed* Pandey*ji,* and he has asked you to come out immediately."

Bibhash follows the *durbaan* to the lobby. He can hear loud, angry voices. He feels cold in the pit of his stomach as he enters.

"There you are," Pandey*ji* says accusingly, "what took you so long? I told you to hurry up so we can rush to the mine."

"Sir, I just went to take a bath, call up the local authorities, and prepare the brief that you had asked for. I—"

"I know, I know," Pandey*ji* says impatiently. "But how long does that take? Now see how agitated these poor workers are. They think the management is not concerned about what's happening. And all this while I've been asking you to hurry up. You speak to them now. I'm sorry, but I refuse to get involved in your internal problems—I have to call the directors."

Bibhash turns to face a crowd of about a dozen workers. He recognizes Shukumar Ghosh, a rabid leftist and the representative of one of the most aggressive unions in the area. "*Han,* Ghosh *da, aapni kamon aachen*?" Bibhash asks sweetly. "How are you? What's all this about?"

"What's this about? You ask me?" Ghosh *da* growls back. "You tell me—what the hell are you doing here, hiding from us?"

"Hiding?" Bibhash acts surprised. "Why should I be hiding? What do you think I am doing here?"

"Well, we really have no idea. You should be out at the pit head with us workers."

Someone pipes up from behind. "And if you don't come right now, we will have to drag you there."

"You don't need to drag me anywhere." Bibhash manages to sound affronted. "I will go as soon as I have tied up all the details with the police and the fire brigade. If they don't arrive on time, we could end up having an avoidable tragedy, and who will take the blame—you?"

"Sooo," Ghosh *da* says slowly, "now that you have spoken to everyone, why don't you come along? Perhaps you will be more useful directing the rescue operation than sitting here making phone calls."

"Yes, yes," Pandey*ji* chimes in happily. "I will take care of all that. Leave that to me and go with them. I will speak to the directors and, if necessary, to the district collector and the superintendent of police—I know them personally. You just leave with them, and I will join you shortly. And, if you have that report ready, please give it to me before leaving."

The crowd of workers closes in around Bibhash as he tries to leave the room. Finally, they allow him to move to his room to fetch the report, with two sturdy fellows escorting him. Bibhash has no intention of trying to run away. He knows that if he as much as makes an attempt, he will be lynched, and Pandey*ji* will not lift a finger to help him—not that he could, even. Bibhash returns, hands over the handwritten report to Pandey*ji*, and is literally pushed out of the room. Everyone clambers into the jeep, and

Bibhash finds himself negotiating the dark, potholed road to the mine for the second time that night. The mood in the vehicle is sullen, and they drive in silence; there is nothing to discuss. The only further information they give Bibhash is that the rescue team led by Balwant has descended twice to Level 3 and made attempts to access Level 2 from different locations, but they've failed in both the attempts. Now one of the pulley winders supporting the skip has developed a snag, and they can use only the fragile cage in further attempts. No one is willing to make a third attempt, as the cage landing on Level 3 is fast inundating. They are awaiting further instructions from Bibhash. Almost everyone is certain that Arif's gang has perished.

Once again Bibhash halts his jeep close to the shaft entry, and the group makes its way to where Balwant is squatting with the team of despondent personnel from the rescue room. The assembled crowd is in an ominous mood, which Bibhash can sense from the jostling he receives as he wades through the laborers.

"Yes, Balwant, what is the position?" Bibhash asks, mustering as much authority in his voice as he can.

"Sir*ji*, we have tried and tried, but we cannot find a place to enter Level Two. Every passage, every incline we tried is flooded under two meters of water. I even tried swimming through it, but I had to give up after a few seconds, when I realized that it got deeper as I progressed. I am the only swimmer, sir*ji*. These boys cannot follow me underwater. I am too old for this sort of thing."

"Don't worry, Balwant, you tried as hard as you could,"

Bibhash says kindly. He is in awe of the mining *sirdar*—what could drive this man? Surely not his salary. "Can I have a look? Is the cage still functional?"

"Sir*ji*, there is at least one meter of water on Level Three, so every time we pull up the winch, the cage has to lift that extra load along with the weight of the people inside. I have noticed a few tears in the winding rope, and the suspension is making strange noises. I don't think it is safe anymore."

A very dark man walks up to them drunkenly and pounces on Bibhash, grabbing him by the collar and launching into a volley of the choicest abuses.

Balwant jumps to Bibhash's aid and disengages them. "Sir*ji*, this is Madho," Balwant explains, "Raimoti's brother. *Oye!* Get back, *bhencho*! Have you gone crazy, like your brother? What do you want?"

On his way to the mine head, to calm himself, Madho guzzled half a bottle of country liquor that his companion was carrying in his pocket. Reluctantly, he steps back from Bibhash.

"*Ai! Ai!* Balwant!" Ghosh *da* intervenes. "Let Madho speak. After all, it is his own brother trapped down there. Let him ask this *sahib* what he proposes to do to rescue Raimoti and the others."

"*Sahib*, I want to know what the management is planning to do," Madho demands, more of the gathered crowd than of Bibhash. "Are we to just sit here on our *gaand* and wait for the bodies to float up to us?"

There is an angry roar from the miners. Someone throws a small stone at Bibhash, which grazes his temple, leaving a red streak.

"Quiet! Quiet!" Bibhash shouts hoarsely at the crowd. "We are doing everything we can to bring the situation under control. I—I have spoken to the concerned authorities, and we will have the police and the fire brigade here within the hour."

"And till then?" someone heckles from the crowd. "Do we just stand here? While Balwant *bhai* and his men have been making repeated trips underground, you have been hiding in the guesthouse, protecting your own arse. Couldn't you have made your calls from the site office here?"

"Calm down! Calm down!" Bibhash pleads. He is fast losing grip on the situation. "I am here now—with you."

"Go fuck your mother!" Ghosh *da* screams, lustily cheered by the crowd. Their leader is taking on the management in style. "We don't need your presence. This is not some marriage that we need a *hijra* to perform for us. We need action!"

The crowd closes in menacingly around the cage landing, and Bibhash feels his bowels turn into water. Just then one of the rescue workers standing near the shaft gives a surprised shout.

"There is someone down there! Look! *Ai!* Who is it?" The man leans into the well and peers down. The crowd surges ahead, and Bibhash is swept along with them. He looks down the deep, dark shaft. He is feeling dizzy and nauseated. Oh God! Indeed, there is someone standing right below the mouth of the shaft in the churningray oval of light cast by the shaft opening. The man is thrashing about in the almost waist-deep water trying to suck him in. His screams rise like wounded partridges and hover, fluttering hopelessly above the heads of the assembled crowd.

"It's Birsa!" someone shouts, recognizing the trapped man.

"He was in Arif's gang—there may be more survivors!" A cheer explodes through the crowd, frightening the partridge away.

"*Oye!* Birsa? Are there others with you?" Balwant leans over to ask. But the roar of the churning river below is too much for them to catch Birsa's answer.

"*Oye!* Hold on—hold on! We are coming down to bring you up. Sir*ji,* we have to send the cage down."

Bibhash is in a daze and doesn't reply. He watches, entranced by the watery dance of death below him. Birsa seems to slip, almost getting swept away, then lunges for the guiding rails of the cage. The rails have been heavily greased, and his fingers grab, slip, then grab again in a desperate attempt at survival. He manages to hang on to a coupling, bobbing like a half-broken twig on the frothingblack water.

The partridge is dead, scythed down by the messengers from Yama who have come to take him away. His screams build up within his head, causing his eyes to bulge with fear and emerge as silent tears.

Bibhash looks down, hypnotized, frozen with shock, and for an instant, meets the pleading white orbs of Birsa's eyes—pearls in crusty shells waiting for a picker.

Rough hands drag Bibhash from the fathomless ocean of dread he has plunged into. They shake him, hoping to bring him back to the land of the living again, but he is sinking . . . sinking . . . sinking. He looks up, his gaze floating over faces, trying to focus on the features contorted in angry disgust. But they are quivering refractions over swirling sands: their shouts no more than dull bubbles. His head spins, and his hands are two buoys, rising slowly in defense against the furious buffeting of fists, but he feels no pain. It is lost in the numbness that fills up the empty spaces inside him.

"He is drunk! *Shaala haaramzada!*" Ghosh *da* says with disgust. "*Boka choda!* What can he do? *Ai!* Ram Babu, Balwant, you send the cage down with someone."

"Ghosh *da,* the cables have frayed," Balwant replies tiredly. "The winder has heated up. The operator tells me that it is unsafe to go down without repairing the cable—it might snap."

"Then repair it quickly." Ghosh *da* has practically taken over the show. He is a born leader, and circumstances have provided him a great opportunity to act as one. "How long will it take?"

"The operator and the technician tell me it will take at least an hour to do the necessary welding, in which time the winder will cool down."

"One hour?" Ghosh *da* asks incredulously. "We don't have that much time, Balwant; Birsa doesn't have that much time. Can't you see how precarious his situation is?"

"But Ghosh *da,* we can't send anyone down—it's too risky. We will end up losing the cage as well as the men. Besides, who will go down?"

"Why," Ghosh *da* says impatiently, "you or any of your boys can make a quick trip, bring out Birsa, and that's it."

"I won't go down now, Ghosh *da,*" Balwant says quietly. "I have been at it for over two hours. My hands are trembling from exertion. I can't risk going all the way down and being unable to pull in Birsa. This cage cannot make another trip for a while. Someone fresh and strong can go."

Ghosh *da* looks around but sees only downcast eyes. He walks into the crowd and asks a few younger men he knows, but they all refuse—everyone is too scared to attempt going down in that cage, especially when they have heard that it could be the last trip down.

What if the cable breaks? No one will be able to go down to bring them out. What if they get swept away? Ghosh *da* exhorts, cajoles, inspires, and threatens, but no one is willing.

"*Arre!* Are all of you women or what?" Ghosh *da* shouts finally, giving up. "Is there no one who will go down and rescue Birsa? You should all drown in shame! *Chchih!*"

"Why don't you go?" A young laborer from Magadh asks. "Can you only do *leaderai*? *Phokusbaji—bas*? Empty words and theatrics—is that all you offer?"

Ghosh *da* hasn't expected this. He is playing to the crowd for effect, so that later, when the blame comes and people start asking why no one saved Birsa, he can turn around and say that he tried to inspire people but they simply failed to rise to the occasion; he will induce guilt and look down from his pedestal, like a true leader should. A leader's life is far too precious. But how does one explain that to these uneducated louts? Suddenly, he gets an inspiration.

"Yes! Why not?" he declares regally. "I will certainly go down— I don't care if I live! At least I will die trying to rescue my brother." He knows that he has at least half a dozen ardent supporters in the crowd who will take the hint and prevent any such foolish attempt. He strides magnificently toward the cage and clambers aboard. "Lower me!" he shouts, looking the image of Veer Hanuman, the brave god depicted in *Ramayana*. "*Joy Bojorong Boli!*"

Predictably, a swarm of supporters descend upon him and try to pull him back. There is a melodramatic scuffle, and Ghosh *da,* a keen amateur stage artist, allows himself to be smothered. His tears are real, though they well from uncontrollable self-appreciation. *Brilliant!* he thinks. *It couldn't have been better had I rehearsed for it.*

"Let me go! Let me go!" he wails loudly, his rich baritone voice ripping easily through the din. "Let me die so Birsa can live!"

"Ghosh *da!*" cries his pet disciple. "You have gone mad. You are too old for this."

"And Birsa is too young to die!" Ghosh *da* replies right on cue. He is starting to enjoy himself. His guru always told him that a great actor must believe in his performance. For a moment Ghosh *da* becomes the great renouncer.

"We can't let you go, *dada*! You mean too much to us."

"All of you mean too much to me—Birsa, too. I have to save him."

"Why should you risk your life when this *harami ka pilla* Mukherjee—that bastard—stands here, dead drunk, not lifting a finger? Doesn't he have some moral responsibility?"

"I can't speak about the moral responsibilities of others," Ghosh *da* declaims righteously. "But I will not stand here and watch my brother die before my eyes. If Mukherjee can live with his conscience, that is truly his good fortune. I can't. It will haunt me for the rest of my life. So let me go."

"No, *dada,*" his loving followers chant in chorus. "Not if Mukherjee doesn't go first. The bloody *hijra*!" The adoring boys take up the chant and turn to Bibhash in an intimidating whorl of raised fists.

"*Hijra! Hijra! Hijra!*" the crowd screams. *Eunuch!*

What? What are they saying? Who are they? Bibhash tries to focus, but the faces are blurred. *Who? Is it Sunita? What is she screaming?* Hijra! Hijra! Hijra! *And Sunita's parents, too? Ha! You never liked me, did you? Thought your daughter married beneath her station—I know what you think of me . . .* Hijra! Hijra! *Who's that? Ma? Where have you come from, Ma? See how they torture your little boy. Look what has become of me*—Hijra! Hijra! *What are you saying, Ma? Your own son?* Hijra! Hijra! Hijra! Baba? *How weak you look—death doesn't suit you—you were always so full of life, so strong. Yes, Baba? What? I can't hear you too well. What did you say?* Hijra! *Not you,* Baba—*you used to love me. You—you were so proud of me—said I was the* cirag *of the family. I cried for days when you died. Oh, I miss you—do you ever think of me? Worry about what has happened to me?* Hijra! Hijra! *What? Haven't I done so much for all of you? Not enough, you say? Too little, you say? How much is enough? How insufficient is too little? Can't you tell that I tried? Really, I did. Is it my fault, Ma, that I failed?* Hijra! Hijra! *Forgive me, Sunita, my love, but I just couldn't do anything more. Do you understand me?* Hijra! Hijra! Hijra! *Ah! That hurts. We've shared so much. All was not well—but everything couldn't have been bad, either. Don't you feel anything for me? Do I mean nothing to you?* Hijra! *Swati, baby. Flesh of my flesh, blood of my blood. Is something the matter? Why are you screaming?* Hijra! Hijra! *Don't you remember how I used to play dolls with you all through summer afternoons when I came home and you were only a toddler?* Hijra! *Beta, don't talk like that—it's bad manners. I want you to know that I tried—couldn't be with you as much as I should have. But I love you.* Hijra! Hijra! *I am sorry, my child.* Hijra! *Your mother just went away—I felt hurt and impotent.* Hijra! *I even wept when I found out, but men shouldn't, I know.* Hijra! Hijra! Hijra! *Don't say that, Beta—I am your father.* Hijra! *Don't you recognize me?* Hijra! Hijra! *Oh! I can't take this anymore. I feel tired. So limp and tired. I can't fight all of you—not anymore.* Hijra! Hijra! Hijra! Hijra!

"I am going down." Bibhash is determined, resolute. The chant subsides abruptly, freezing into brittle blocks of doubtful silence. Bibhash walks slowly toward the cage, and the crowd disperses before him. He climbs into the contraption and nods at Balwant.

"Sir*ji*, it's really not—"

"Start the winder, Balwant. We don't have time."

Bibhash is feeling quite relaxed and relieved. Lines from some yellowing pages talk to him like old lovers. Sometimes like enemies. *In my end is my beginning.* A sonorous voice drawls in his ears. *Why do they look so somber? It's not a cremation, for there is no pyre. There's only water. And waiting pearls. Or are they eyes? And why are they so restive?* the voice asks, surprising him. *Be still and let me enter darkness—that will be the darkness of redemption, and through that darkness shall I see light.* Bibhash looks down the black hole and sees light. Birsa looks up to him and can see only a dark cloud. The motor starts with a hum, and the cage descends hesitantly into the shaft.

As he moves away from the surface, Bibhash feels a calm envelop him. He thinks he has been too much in the sun. He has been scorched and blinded by the brightness of the world. His heart seeks darkness with an eagerness that is almost painful. It is getting dark, dark, dark, and he finally sees a ray of hope. *Here is a place of un-being hidden from the groping sunbeams of the past.* The voice has changed and sounds more high-pitched and insistent. *Darkness fuses effortlessly into light, and reality softly blends into the unreal. Amorphous shadows dance nimbly around me, creating forms out of nothingness—building a future that will never exist.* Now the voice dips into a rasping whisper full of sadness and foreboding. *This is a forge where perception and sensibility are melted, hammered, and twisted, creating a new awareness of being.* Bibhash is anxious but prepared for that newness.

Birsa has to let go of the guide rails as the cage comes down. He does so with fear. He has seen the might of the black river gouging its path through the netherworld. His gnarled fingers release the rails, and he clings to the beam of light from Bibhash's headlamp. Cold fear rises up to his chest in waves as he waits for the cage to descend to the landing. He has seen Lakhan and Sagan sucked away by the wild waters, even as he tried hard to pry their limp bodies away from their souls. But the two were inseparably fused, and in the end, he had to let both go, whispering a prayer in their wake.

Chchappak! Gglugg! The cage lands heavily on the steel landing and stays there, swaying gently like a boat in turbulent water. Birsa wants to jump and grab the hands extended to him, but he has no legs—there is only water below his chest. He tries to reach out with his hands, but he has no arms—there is only air above his chest. So long, so long in water that he is melting, mingling inexorably into the river. His legs are twin currents trying impatiently to move away with the flow: waves unto waves, water to water.

"Give me your hands!" Bibhash roars above the sound of the

water. Birsa can only stare helplessly and shake his head. Bibhash tries to lean out but fails to reach Birsa, who is by now more water than man. In a deliberate, calm action, Bibhash jumps off the cage and grabs Birsa by the hair, holding the safety bar with his other hand. He had not anticipated the force with which the gushing water is trying to claim them. He falters briefly, his feet slipping on the uneven submerged floor of the tunnel, but he manages to pull Birsa toward him, inch by excruciating inch. For the moment nothing else exists—nothing matters. It is just life against death, struggle against surrender, Bibhash against himself.

Slowly, ever so slowly, Bibhash pushes the dissipating fluidity of Birsa toward the cage. Birsa offers no assistance—he can't—and inertly allows himself to be moved. Bibhash returns to the cage with Birsa, and the two stand there for an interminable moment, panting and retching. Then Bibhash bends down to hold Birsa by the waist and gives a mighty shove. Birsa slides over the edge of the cage landing and flops on the cage floor in a paralyzed heap. He is all water below his nostrils. With an effort, he reaches out his hand, and Bibhash holds it in acknowledgment of Birsa's gratitude.

Gently, Bibhash breaks Birsa's grip and presses the large green button on the control panel. The cage shudders like a reluctant bullock then slowly lifts through the water. The cables creak and groan with the effort of rising against the ruthless force of water, but the cage continues its ascent. Bibhash lets go of the safety bar and stands still in shoulder-deep water. Birsa jerks his head up to look at Bibhash in disbelief. Still no sound comes out of his throat. The cage at last lifts clear of the water and starts creaking its way up the rails. Birsa looks down at Bibhash's face, floating on the water, looking so peaceful and happy. He blinks the water out of his eyes. When he looks again, the face is gone. Only bubbles remain where Bibhash was.

Trahi mam! Trahi mam! Trahi mam!
Save me!

chapter 6

A smokygray drizzle wafts down from the starless night sky, fluttering like an immense lace curtain across the dimly lit streets of the township, adding a ghostly feel to the nightscape. Madho speeds through the slushy bylanes on his scooter, eager to share the news with Dolly. He is almost sober, after spending a couple of hours at the pit head, shaken and deeply disturbed by the sight he witnessed there. Death has never been a novelty in his life, but watching the manner in which Bibhash surrendered his life has stirred indescribable thoughts of gloom in his heart. How can a man be so ruthless about his own life? How can one be so devoid of a will to survive?

They were all peering down the shaft, watching the entire event in the surreal light of a searchlight someone had rigged up. They saw Bibhash rescue Birsa and safely deposit him in the cage, and then they all watched with disbelieving eyes as Bibhash calmly stepped away after pushing the button. Bibhash barely resisted when the currents sucked him under the surface. He went down without a cry. Birsa emerged from the jaws of death in a state of complete shock, unable to utter a word about what had happened. The doctor present declared that some water had entered Birsa's lungs and he would probably need to be operated upon, but he would survive—though whether the paralysis was temporary still needed to be determined. They had rushed him off in a jeep to the field hospital about twenty kilometers away. Madho left soon after the police and a couple of fire tenders arrived on the scene in a belated answer to the frantic calls made to the civic authorities.

Madho parks his Bajaj Chetak scooter at the narrow entrance of the depressing yellow four-story block of company-provided flats for lower-level executives. At least it is much more respectable than the hut where they lived till he was promoted four years ago. His flat is on the ground floor, with a garbage-strewn patch of a garden that no one bothers to maintain. The only evidence of human involvement in this ugly weed-infested patch are a few flourishing *tulsi* plants in a little brick-lined enclosure. Raimoti is obsessive about his attachment to the shrubs and makes it a point to water them every evening. Some days, when he is too tired or stoned, Tina tends to the beloved shrubs. Madho notices that the *tulsi* leaves are looking particularly bright green this night. He feels a cold shiver down his spine and knocks at the termite-eaten plywood door.

"What took you so long?" Dolly asks petulantly, opening the door. "I have had my dinner, so now you will need to have yours cold."

"Six people have died. They drowned in Mine Number Three!"

"If you want, Tina can heat up the fish—she is still awake."

"Raimoti was with the gang that perished."

"Really?" Dolly stops in her tracks, suddenly interested. "Are you certain?"

"Yes. There were six men in that gang. Only one survived. The subarea manager, Mukherjee, died saving him. I was there when the last man, Birsa, came up. The mine has flooded completely to the uppermost level. There is no way anyone on the lower levels could have survived."

He hears a gasp and turns to find Tina standing at the door to the second bedroom. Her eyes are puffyred from hours of weeping in silence. Madho feels an irrational urge to slap her, but he refrains. Tina has too much of her ill-omened mother and her mad uncle in her. Sometimes Madho has doubts that there is any of him in his younger daughter.

"But what about the bodies? Have they managed to retrieve any?" asks Dolly.

"No, not yet," Madho replies tiredly. "They will first have to pump out the water before someone can go down to search for the bodies. That might take a couple of days, at least. I hear they have put eight pumps on the job, which will work round-the-clock for the next few days."

"But what if some of those five have managed to survive and are trapped underground—what if Raimoti has survived?" Dolly asks warily.

"Not a chance," Madho says, shaking his head and sighing. "I saw the condition below with my own eyes. The force of the water was so much that Mukherjee was literally swept away in the blink of an eye. No one can survive that."

Tina bursts into a stifled sob and rushes back into her room. Madho slumps on the sofa, unbuttoning his drenched shirt, lost in his thoughts. Dolly stands behind him for a moment, then goes to the bathroom, brings a towel, and lovingly starts to pat him dry. Madho looks up in surprise but doesn't say anything. They sit in silence for a while, and then Madho goes to the bedroom to change into dry clothes.

Dolly excitedly springs into action and takes out the barely touched bottle of rum from that evening. She gets out a couple of glasses, some ice in a bowl, and some fried fish leftovers from dinner. She is ready by the time Madho emerges from the bedroom. He sits down quietly on the sofa and lights up a cigarette. Dolly hands him an ashtray and pours a stiff measure of rum into his glass. She adds some ice and hands over the glass; Madho grasps it without a word and sits there morosely, holding the glass. They can hear Tina's sobs from the other room.

"Shut up!" Madho shouts, turning toward Tina's room. "Stop that stupid noise, or I will come and give you a tight slap."

The sobbing stops almost instantly.

"*O, mera jaanu*—my darling," Dolly croons softly. "Don't let that silly girl bother you. Here, have your drink. It will calm you down, my poor husband. How tired you must be; you haven't even eaten anything. Have some fish—I've heated it for you."

Madho takes a deep swallow, then another. His mind is in a whirl. It is not as if he is very attached to Raimoti. On the contrary, the two barely speak. Raimoti is the antithesis of all that Madho believes in. Madho believes in himself; Raimoti is a believer in cosmic power. For Madho, ambition and betterment mean everything; Raimoti is impervious to such thoughts. For years now Madho has struggled, fought against odds, and risen slowly up the social ladder. For decades Raimoti has vegetated, drifted, and sunk into the mire of social oblivion. It always intrigues Madho how, despite his distinctive antisocial behavior, Raimoti always appears to have a clutch of what can only be termed as *followers*. He is a laughable but popular figure among the simple laborers of the mining community.

Take Arif, for example. The man is positively criminal. But he seems to have an inexplicable fascination with Raimoti's strangeness. The two are inseparable on their off evenings, and Madho has often spied them under the great *neem* tree, near the Pir Baba's *dargah,* sitting on a cot with the battered harmonium, surrounded by a bunch of malingering laborers. On the rare occasions when Madho has stopped by to listen to what is going on, he has been surprised to hear Raimoti singing *bhajans* and *sufi naaths* and discoursing on life. Imagine, a lunatic like Raimoti discoursing on life! But people seem to enjoy it. True, it is not like a set of disciples listening to their guru—there is too much ganja- and *afim*-induced bonhomie for that—but Raimoti appears to be the cynosure of such stoned gatherings.

There is something else Raimoti is famous for—something that has earned him the epithet *tulsi baba*. Raimoti is a popular quack. Every Tuesday morning, before sunrise, he sits under the *neem* tree, listening to confessions of unmentionable and incurable maladies of the local villagers, doling out doses of remedies wrapped in leaves and some homilies on existence. Madho is not sure how effective these prescriptions are, but there is always a re-

spectable crowd at that unearthly hour to convince him of the gull-
ibility of the villagers. Raimoti professes great faith in the healing
properties of the herb, and people believe that his formulations are
prepared primarily from *tulsi*. Knowing Raimoti and considering
the addicted throngs of patients, Madho suspects there must be a
fair infusion of extracts from cannabis and belladonna.

Madho is dismissive of his brother's mystical manifestations.
He has made a few attempts in the past to discourage this streak
of spiritual vagabondage in Raimoti, but each time his suggestions
have been met with an aggressive sullenness till Madho has learned
where to draw the line. He minds his own business and lets Raimoti go about his.

Unlike Dolly, Madho does not really dislike Raimoti; he is
more impatient than disgusted with his brother. After all, Madho
still remembers the time when, for a few years, Raimoti was the
only earning member of their family. Their father was too old and
sick to do anything more productive than consume copious quantities of toddy and sit around the whole day in the dubious company
of like-minded geriatrics. Raimoti would work overtime, pushing
himself to the extreme to earn the few extra rupees that kept the
family going. Slowly, Raimoti married off two of his sisters and put
Madho through school.

Raimoti's own marriage was a disaster from the start. Dulari,
his wife, was an extremely social woman by local standards, some-
what along the lines of Madho's own wife. She possessed a kind of
restless attraction that resulted in six perpetually bawling children
for Raimoti and a string of admirers for Dulari. Dulari was educated—tenth-pass—and one of her paramours, a social activist,

involved her in adult education programs in the district. Raimoti protested vaguely, but that was not enough to deter Dulari. Her work required travel, and at times she would be away for as long as a week. When Dulari began bringing home toys for the children and clothes for Madho and Raimoti's father, Raimoti realized that social service paid well. She never got anything for Raimoti, as a statement of her disregard.

Soon after their sixth baby, Dulari declared that she didn't want any more children. It was difficult for Raimoti to comprehend what she meant, because he was convinced of the irrepressibility of procreation. Dulari tried to explain the concept of contraception to her doubtful husband, who was aghast at the idea of wearing a rubber sheath as a receptacle for his seed. He found the idea repulsive and against the laws of nature. But Dulari persevered and finally convinced Raimoti to get a vasectomy done in a *nasbandi* camp organized by the village women's welfare group, the *Mahila Jagaran Manch*. Raimoti agreed because by then he had lost interest in sex. He had discovered the joys of *hadia*.

Being the youngest of the siblings, Madho was always a little in awe of Raimoti. He was impressed with the ease with which his quiet brother could slaughter and skin a chicken or a pig. Raimoti had a matter-of-fact approach toward killing and death that scared Madho. In his childhood and adolescence, Madho was never shy of approaching his big brother to complain about some bully. On one such occasion, Madho remembered, Raimoti dragged the bully by his balls, dunked him in the buffalo pond, and held him underwater till the fellow had almost stopped thrashing about. Only then did Raimoti release the hapless teenager and drain the slimy water from his lungs. The bully never even looked at Madho after that. This unpredictable side unnerves Madho, even at his age. One can never truly know how Raimoti will react in a given situation.

After Dulari decided to run away with a truck driver one morning, Raimoti vanished for a week. He returned home with a couple of tattered books and a mystical expression. Raimoti is literate, but the only things Madho has ever seen him read are these books—he doesn't even read the newspaper. When asked, Raimoti simply said that he had gone away with a *sadhu,* an ascetic, and met God. After this divine interaction, the *sadhu* found it befitting for Raimoti to have a copy of the revered scriptures. The *sadhu* also gave Raimoti two other boons: a lifelong addiction to ganja and a packet of *tulsi* seeds. For the next several months, Raimoti did not speak a word to anyone. He went underground and came out to drink *hadia,* smoke ganja, and eat *tulsi* leaves while he sat in a corner of their tenement reading one or the other of his precious books. His family was convinced that he had gone mad.

When Madho turned sixteen, Raimoti got him a job in the mines. Strangely, people listened to him in those days. Gradually, Raimoti's six children grew up, died, or got married and went away. Raimoti met each of these eventualities with a disconcerting equanimity that frightened Madho. Slowly, Raimoti became almost detached from the world and its vicissitudes. He became a fleeting presence in the house, and Madho came to expect his inaccessibility. Madho also started to get angry about Raimoti's remarkable lack of ambition to achieve anything in life. The brothers started drifting apart in more ways than one, and Raimoti descended deeper into the chaos within his own soul.

When their father died at the astonishing age of 103, by all reliable accounts, the intensity of Raimoti's psychotropic daze worsened. The death of his last son in a mining disaster seemed to put Raimoti irretrievably on the other side of sanity. That was when the Beast, which had been incubating for years in Raimoti's mind, came to life. Madho made some halfhearted attempts to bring his brother back into the realm of the normal, but there was too much distance to cover. So Madho continued leading his own life the best he could, marrying, having children, remarrying, and settling down to a progressive existence.

Over the years, the brothers have drifted apart, but today, when Madho is almost certain that Raimoti has perished in the flood of Mine Number 3, he somehow cannot feel the same thrill of relief and release that his wife does. In fact, it is difficult for him to accept that Raimoti could be dead. Good or bad, sane or not, Raimoti is, after all, his own blood. He knows that Raimoti is more of a nuisance than a use at home, but there is something reassuring about his disturbing presence. Perhaps it is only a hangover from his childhood, as Dolly keeps pointing out. Perhaps, after all, it is good riddance to bad rubbish. Madho feels a pinch of guilt at his thoughts.

In contrast, Dolly is rather delirious with suppressed joy. She comes from a matriarchal lineage in which men have their uses but not the significance that they enjoy in these parts. She simply can't understand why anyone should mourn the loss of a life that had long lost relevance, except in terms of monthly income. She knows that she eventually would have succeeded in separating the brothers, but it would have been a long and tedious battle. Madho is too much in awe of his older brother. This propitious development has obviated the necessity for a long-drawn battle of wits with her husband. Now they can get on with their lives, free from the maddening penumbra of Raimoti, his morbid spiritualism, his hallucinations, and his Beast. She feels grateful for this unexpected bounty of destiny, but she knows that now is not the time to express it.

"*Ai*, Madho," Dolly asks, pouting, "why don't you have some fish, man? An empty stomach won't increase the chances of Raimoti's survival, will it?"

"Dolly," Madho replies irritably, "how can I sit here eating fried fish when I know that my own brother could have just died?"

"I realize, man"—Dolly is the picture of commiseration—"but fasting will be of no use. If you fall sick, what good will it do? Here, let me feed my darling."

"*Bas, bas*—enough!" Madho stops Dolly from stuffing his mouth with fish. He takes a few gulps of the rum to wash it down.

Dolly pours herself a drink and sips carefully. She needs her wits about her. "So," she asks, trying to sound casual, "what happens if—God forbid—Raimoti is no longer with us in this world? How will they be sure?"

"Like I told you," Madho says morosely, "I am almost certain that he is—that he is dead. He couldn't have survived that inundation—he is so old—was! Birsa was the sturdiest member of the gang, and I saw the condition he came out in. He is barely alive. I shudder to imagine how the others must have died in that underground grave."

"But surely the company must have some laid-down procedures for this kind of a thing."

"Yes, they do," Madho replies flatly, recalling the information
given by the subarea office clerks. "They send a team down after
the water has been pumped out, if that is possible. They retrieve
the bodies and hand them over to the police for an autopsy—that's
more of a formality in such cases. Then a death certificate is drawn,
and the company strikes the name off the rolls. That's it."

"And then?"

"Then what?" Madho asks uneasily.

"Well, what about compensation, benefits, and all that?"

"Yeah, they work all that out."

"Ah! And how much time does that usually take?"

"Oh, I don't know." Madho is getting agitated with all this
questioning. "I haven't ever claimed all this before, have I?"

"*Arre!* The fish is gone," Dolly says quickly, "let me bring
some more from the kitchen. There is also some pork from last
night. I will quickly heat it up and get it for you while you decide
what to do."

Madho wonders what there is to decide. *There is nothing I
can do,* he thinks bitterly. *Raimoti has done it all by himself.* Madho
is suddenly aware of someone standing behind him and looks up.
Tina is standing with a forlorn expression, looking half scared and
half determined.

"What is it, Tina?" he asks ill-humoredly.

"Papa—"

"Yes? What do you want? For God's sake, don't just stand
there looking like a ghost—say what you want!"

"Papa—is *kaku* . . ."

"What? What about your *kaku*?"

"Is he—is he—I mean, I heard you tell that—"

"Yes!" Madho says brutally. "He is dead. Now are you satisfied? Go back to your room and leave me alone. Don't bother us now—we are discussing important things. When you wake up in the morning, you can ask all the questions you want from your mummy."

"B-but, Papa—have you seen the b-body?"

"What?" Madho shouts angrily. "What sort of a question is that? No. I haven't seen the body, but I hope it has been washed away for good. Go now!"

Tina looks baffled and hurt by this outburst. She doesn't understand many things that go on around her, and this seems to be one of them. She stands there a little longer, but her father's increasingly violent expression scares her, and she quietly goes back to her room. Madho returns to his reverie and refills his glass. At least he can drink to his fill. Tomorrow is not a working day.

"Was that Tina?" Dolly asks nonchalantly, coming out of the kitchen with a tray of food, which she sets on the coffee table. Madho just nods glumly.

"That girl worries me at times. She is so much like Raimoti in some ways, it's eerie."

"He's her uncle," Madho says defensively.

"I know. That is why it worries me." Dolly leaves it at that. She puts some fried fish on a quarter plate and settles down with her glass. "So, you were telling me . . ." she starts.

"About what?"

"Oh, about the formalities after—after an accident like this."

"Well, I will go down to the office tomorrow and find out."

"But isn't there some sort of compensation that they give immediately to the bereaved family?" Dolly persists.

"Yes, there is. Then there are dues, gratuity, insurance, and such other things. I have to find out."

"I don't want you to exert yourself. I'm sure things will get sorted out soon enough for . . ."

"For what?" Madho asks suspiciously.

"Oh! It's just that I know how much that house matters to you—to all of us. It would have taken us years to save up the money—but now . . ."

"What do you mean?"

"Well, if—if the compensation is anything reasonable, our problem should be . . . solved. No?"

"You forget that Raimoti has living children—four of them," Madho growls.

"Oh! I know," Dolly says smoothly, "but they are all girls, aren't they? And married for years. They are no longer dependents. Everyone here knows that we took care of Raimoti."

"He didn't need anyone to take care of him."

"Yes, but he did live in this house, didn't he?"

"If sleeping in the drawing room and having a few meals a week in this house amounts to that, then yes."

"What's wrong with you?" Dolly says crossly. "I am only trying to be realistic about things, and you are sounding so terse and rude."

"Dolly, I have just lost my brother!"

"Wrong—you have been losing him over the years. In fact, he was not all there. What you saw wasn't the Raimoti you are mourning for now; it was the memory of what he used to be years ago. He was more dead than alive—you know that. If not the mines, the drugs would have gotten him soon enough. So what is there to mourn about? You knew he didn't have too long to live, the way he carried on. And what did he care for you? He rarely even spoke to you. The only one he seemed to care for in this house was Tina, who you say is your daughter. Well, I have my doubts!"

"Dolly!"

"Sorry, I don't mean to hurt you. I just want to shake you up so you can see things in the right perspective. Do you put it beyond Raimoti that one fine morning you would have woken up to find that he had disappeared—that he had gone away with another holy man up into the mountains? Or that he'd declared out of the blue that from that day he would live under the *neem* tree near the *dargah*? Can you say that he was normal, predictable?"

Madho is silent. He knows Dolly is right. Raimoti could have done all that and more. "What's the point, Dolly?"

"The point, dear Madho," Dolly says sweetly, "is that you must be aware of the situation and be ready to respond correctly when the moment comes."

"I fail to understand your twisted logic, so please say exactly what you mean."

"I mean—that it is more or less certain that Raimoti is—well, dead."

"So?"

"So, there are some benefits that will accrue out of his death, whether we mourn for him or not."

"Most certainly. So?"

"Those benefits will make people greedy—I mean Raimoti's daughters. I know how fast such news travels. Once they hear about the compensation, they are sure to descend upon us, claiming their share, if not the entire amount. Why should we let them do that? You must be prepared, and we will claim the compensation as early as possible and invest it before anyone can raise a controversy over it. Once it's invested, we can relax and fight out the claims at our leisure. At least we would have gotten it out of the company."

"How can we do that? Raimoti's children have a legitimate claim."

"Who cares about legitimacy? Where were they when Raimoti was burdening our lives?"

"I never felt he was a burden."

"Sure. I am the selfish, mean one around here. I am the vamp. If you were so happy about Raimoti, why didn't you go and sit with him under that *neem* tree in the evenings? Why didn't you take his *tulsi* medicines? Why didn't you enjoy his harmonium? Why did you think he was crazy? Why did you treat him like a pariah in your house? No, Madho, I refuse to take the exclusive blame of not treating your brother right. If I am guilty of it, so are you. And don't delude yourself that it is otherwise!"

"Say what you have to say and be done with it."

"Yes, that is what I intend to do—say what I have to say and then leave the final choice with you. All I am saying is that Raimoti is dead. We have as much claim over any benefits that arise out of his death as his own children—in fact, I feel that our claim is stronger, but I won't argue that point just yet. Don't let sentiment and foolish ethics get involved. It is going to be a race. Whoever claims the benefits first will be in an advantageous position. Since you are working in Kariakhani and Raimoti's daughters are elsewhere, take that advantage and put in your claim. There is nothing wrong with that. We will hope that it is processed and granted to us in absence of any other claim. I am sure it can be managed if we try. There, I have had my say. Now it is entirely up to you."

Madho is quiet for a long time. He doesn't have a queasy conscience. But he is uncomfortable with the idea of cheating Raimoti's children—not that what Dolly proposes will be tantamount to cheating, really. After all, no one would deny that Raimoti lived with them. Similarly, no one would say that Raimoti's daughters ever bothered about him. Besides, any cash benefit would come in handy for the house they have been dreaming of for so many years. But going about it so slyly, even before informing his nieces, is not completely aboveboard. It is not pangs of conscience that he is having—it is fear of retribution at the hands of Raimoti's spirit that weighs on his mind. There was that slightly supernatural element in his brother's complex personality that troubles Madho and makes him worry about the consequences of messing around with Raimoti's spirit. But he can't talk about any of that with Dolly—that will only lay him open to her ridicule.

"Okay," he says finally. "I will wait till the official release is out before I inform Raimoti's daughters by post. In the meantime,

I am sure there will be some interim cash compensation. I will claim that. I am known to Ghosh *da* as well as the *babus* in the chief GM's office. No one will object to it."

"Great!" Dolly says with obvious relief. "You really are smart! All you need is a little inspiration from time to time to keep you heading in the right direction. So let's drink to your commendable decision!"

They drink in silence for a while and think their dark individual thoughts. Dolly feels that she has just won a lottery, and it seems that many of her problems will get solved. For the first time in this house, she feels a tinge of endearment for her dead brother-in-law. She smiles softly at the thought of having a *tulsi* shrub in their new house as a memorial to her benefactor.

Madho, a man of action and great ambition, is quickly lost in calculations of interest on deposit and equated monthly installments for his house. They sit there, quietly enjoying their respective visions of happiness, while Tina sits in her room next to the window, turned away from the sleeping forms of her sister, Mona, and stepbrother, Tommy, who briefly woke up when Madho returned but have gone back to deep sleep after a quick bout of mutual masturbation. They are at it whenever possible and have threatened Tina with dire consequences if she squeals on them. They needn't—she really doesn't care as long as they leave her alone. Once when she was half asleep, Tommy tried to feel her up. She turned to him with a coy smile, and he stretched out his arms, sensing conquest. The kick in his groin was excruciating and worse for not being able to scream for fear of waking up his mother in the next room. He never tried it again.

Tina just wants a life away from her stifling home and family, all except her dear *kaku* Raimoti.

There is another knock on the door, and Tina hears her father get up to open it. She hopes against reason that it is her *kaku*, that they've all been mistaken, that Raimoti has somehow escaped death and returned. But it is someone from the manager's office. She can hear the brief conversation quite clearly.

"*Han?* Prasad*ji*? At this time?" Madho asks, a little peeved at this interruption of his profitable calculations.

"Sorry, Madho—I feel really bad about Raimoti. He was a good man. But I am here to tell you that the GM of personnel has called you—he has called the nearest relatives of all those who have been injured or are feared drowned tonight. So please come quickly. I have a jeep waiting around the corner, picking up a few others."

"But why?"

"*Arre!* GM *sahib* wants to discuss some matters relating to compensation. He wants to talk to all the affected families in private first."

"Oh! Okay! I am coming with you, but I will take my own scooter. Dolly! Lock the door after me."

They are gone.

Tina has heard most of the discussion between her father and Dolly. She hears her father start his scooter and leave. She sits there silently, leaning on Raimoti's harmonium, sobbing and listening to the dull patter of rain against the windowpane.

chapter 7

Water. Black coal. And a little air. There is silence where no sound has been. Silence where no sound may be. In this cold grave under the earth, no voice is hushed, no life treads silently. Only Raimoti and Arif, anchored silently on the dead waters of this remorseless river. Unstirred by death, unmoving in life. Thin, musty air hangs heavily above them like a canopy against death. Two birds of the same kind and inseparable by destiny cling to the same tree. One eats the fruit, the other looks on in patient hope.

I sit on the ledge, immersed in sorrow, grieving my own impotence, but when I see Arif hanging from my knees and realize his glory, my grief diminishes.

It is so cold.

From chaos the universe was born, from void came life. From the abyss of despair came the spirit of survival. Flowers from earth. Gold from fire. I burn like fire. Little flames bloom first at my toes, then my stomach, then my heart. Now my soul is on fire. Do you feel the heat?

It is so cold in the water.

See the glow. Feel the radiating warmth. Can you feel?

I see nothing. It's so dark. I feel nothing. Benumbed.

In the beginning there was nothing. You are back where you started. Before One there was Zero. Nothing. Death—it covered everything.

I am hungry.

Hunger is death. Like death, it dwells in your mind. It is nothing. From nothing He created the Mind. Thirsty Mind. From that Mind came water. I know it—so water comes to me. The froth of this water encrusted to form the earth. Then He rested. From Him, thus rested and warmed, came forth His essence and radiance. Fire. Feel the heat within.

It's so cold. I'm hungry. I am tired. I am scared.

You are not alone. I see two birds on this tree.

I see nothing.

You are not blind. You only have your eyes open. Shut your eyes and you shall see.

My eyes have turned to water. Everything has turned to water. I am still hungry. Too hungry.

Water is greater than food. Water is everything. Without water, there is no life. It is water that assumes different forms of this earth, the atmosphere, the mountains, the sky, the gods, the men, the grass, the trees, the worms, the insects, the birds, and the Beast. Meditate on water. There lies your deliverance.

I am one with water. It takes away my life.

You do not die in water, you become rich in water. You become what you are made of. He who is within the water, whom water does not know but whose body has become water, controls the water from within.

It is cold. I understand nothing. I can't speak anymore.

There must not be silence. Silence is Death. Know the importance of Sound.

Tell me. What else is there to do but listen? I feel deaf.

Hau *is this World;* hai *is Air;* i *is Fire;* ya *is Food;* iha *is Self;* hum *is the variable interjectional sound; breath is Sound.*

Chchapp! Glugg! What's that?

The Sound of Water.

It is all around me. I shiver. Why do I feel breathless?

Consider this: When He produced the senses, they quarreled with one another. Death, in its manifestation of weariness, laid hold of them, slowly smothering each. But Death could not conquer that which we call Breath. All the senses agreed, therefore, that Breath was the greatest among them. They all acquired its form. Intangible but real. These are seven hostile kinsmen of Breath. Hostile because they hinder the perception of the inner self. You feel breathless because you have allowed these hostile sensualities to cloud your perception. Converge all thoughts on Breath. Breathe in and breathe out and wish Let not Death claim me. *You will vanquish Death.*

How long? How long can one go on just breathing?

Each being comes with a finite number of Breaths, both inward and outward. Conserve these and you breathe longer. Fritter them and you perish.

Why should I die? Why here? Why now? Why us?

Forget me. I am neither dead nor alive. Neither here nor elsewhere. For me, existence is merely a sum of the past and the future and both intersect to form the present. All is irredeemable for me. I am here because this is where I am meant to be now. All roads of my life, from time past, present, and future, converge here. I am here in quest of the Beast. Our paths shall cross here.

But I don't want to die.

Why do you want to live?

Who wants to die?

He who has finished the business of his life. When you come to the end of a book, the only thing you can do is shut it.

I haven't finished the business of my life yet.

That is what I asked—why do you want to live? What unfinished business do you have?

I am young.

That is not an end, neither an excuse for living.

I am unmarried.

You see that as an achievement or a failure?

Everyone marries. Marries and has children. That is how life goes on. I still feel so cold.

Life goes on regardless. He finds His own ways to perpetuate life. Marriage is not His preferred instrument for that. It is both above and beneath life.

You say so. You've been through it all—had a wife, a family, and children.

A wife—ardhangini—I shared only one half. A family as thick as the air we breathe. Children, who have sprouted, fructified, and withered away.

But I have to experience it yet.

What is experience?

I experience hunger. I experience cold. I experience fear.

Those are perceptions. The sum total of perceptions is experience. Perceptions can be attributive. Experiences are neither good nor bad.

I still don't have them. My life is incomplete.

What will complete it?

Inheritance. Someone to carry my name when I am gone. Someone created by me and offered to this world.

What do you know of creation?

I exist. I am going numb.

Truly. That is the first tenet of creation. I am. Therefore I exist. But you might say that there is no delight in being alone. So He caused His solitary Self to split into two. From the conjugation of the split halves arose a third, which split to form the fourth. And so it continued. That is the genesis of lineage. That is the tree of life. The fear of aloneness is the root of the desire for inheritance. The fear of mortality is the root of the desire for children. You want to leave your footprints on the sands of time.

My feet are dead. If there were sand, I would like to leave footprints. But there is no sand. There is only water.

When you have traversed the path, what do the footprints matter?

If none of this matters, then why does anyone live?

Because He created them so that they live. He has His own reasons; we men devise our own.

You mean this life has no meaning?

It surely has, but most of us have yet to discover its significance in His grand scheme.

And if you can't do that before you die?

You will get another chance.

I don't believe in rebirths.

Neither do I. But do you believe in One Consciousness? The Almighty?

Yes. I feel weak.

Is there anything outside the Omnipotent, the Omniscient, the Omnipresent?

Nothing.

Then everything that exists comes from that Being? Everything returns unto It?

I think so. But I am hungry.

Then if everything comes from that Source, and if there is nothing outside It, we shall always exist in that Eternity. You can discover what you like, when you like, in that Eternity. You don't need a rebirth.

You mean in Afterlife?

If life is so isolated, so separate, what lies after? What goes before? Is it distinct from the Eternal existence of the Almighty?

You tell me. You are the one who chews *tulsi* and smokes ganja.

Want some? I have it here in this pouch. Let me light it.

You are crazy. We will suffocate.

Not if we die first.

I will suffocate to death.

Not if you drown first.

Do what you feel like. I don't care. I am tired.

Tell me, if I can show the way out, will your life change?

Try me. I shall be a new man.

In what way? Are you unhappy about what you are?

Yes.

And yet you want to continue this existence.

That is different. Your crazy mind will not understand.

Try me.

Another chance, and I will do things differently. Live life differently.

Explain.

I will do only good and keep away from sins.

I never realized you were so guilt-ridden.

We are all sinners. You, too, O crazy saint. Yes, I have guilt. I want to undo the sins committed—do the good things omitted.

That presupposes complete comprehension of goodness. Goodness is distinct from pleasantness. Do you have the discretion to differentiate between what is pleasant and what is good? Even if you have the discretion, do you have the determination to always choose good over the pleasant? Even if you have the determination, will destiny permit that?

I feel claustrophobic. If I get out alive, I will have the discretion, and I shall have the determination.

Indeed, then you will be a wise man. But there are times when even a wise man has to bow to the force of circumstance and do what he knows is wrong.

Knowingly, I will never do wrong. That is my promise to the Almighty, if He gets me out.

Sounds more like a deal to me. What if I tell you of a situation and ask you to reply truthfully about what you will do?

Go ahead.

Suppose you get out. You become a good man. You get married and have children. One day your cherished son falls sick. You need money for the treatment, otherwise he will die. It is your moral duty to do your best to save your child. On your way home, you see a commotion in the street. A robber is running away with loot from a prosperous shop. You chase him and apprehend him in a dark alley where there is no one else. He offers to give you half the booty if you let him go. A substantial amount. Will you strike a bargain?

My head hurts.

Dilemma always hurts. Tell me—what will you do?

I will take the booty and save my son. So would you or anyone else in the circumstances.

Perhaps. But would that not be abetting the robber? Would you not share the moral burden of that crime?

I will. But the Almighty will understand. It will be deciding about a life or death. I would have no choice. There will be no sin.

Wrong. You always have a choice. Your action will always remain sinful. It is the price that you are prepared to pay for the right choice that matters. What matters is where you draw the line. Will it be only to save your son's life or also for his education or for his comfort or for the pure pleasure of being rich? They are all reasons enough to make one strike a deal with the robber. So what you are saying is that if you think there is justification enough, you will do what you know is wrong. That is what I meant when I asked if you have the discretion and the determination to walk on the right path in adversities.

I will learn. Just get me out.

I am sure you will learn—if you want to. So if you want to make a pact with the Almighty, say that you will try to learn to differentiate between right and wrong, good and evil. Don't say you will do that. There can be insurmountable obstructions. Don't cheat your God.

You tire me.

Realization is tiresome. A puff of this excellent ganja will rejuvenate you.

No. Addictions are evil.

Then why are you addicted to life?

Oh! I am going to kill you.

Remember, I am already dead.

You are nuts. Why do I feel a pain in my chest?

Try to breathe air, not water. The pain will go.

Not easy, hanging from your shuddering old bones in this water, is it?

Come. I shall not trouble you more. We will talk about other things now.

I don't want to talk. My tongue is turning to water. Why don't you pray for us? You are the enlightened one. Perhaps God will listen to you.

A prayer is the cry of a lost soul. I have my bearings right. He knows about us. He wants me to be here to confront the Beast and vanquish it. I have to be patient.

I can see no reason why He wants me to be here with you. I have no Beast to fight.

We all do. There is a Beast for all of us. I have discovered mine. You still have to find yours. But it already exists.

What is your Beast?

I have never told anyone, but you deserve to know. It is Fear.

Fear of what?

Fear of Death.

I thought you were not afraid of dying.

But I am afraid of Death.

What is the difference?

Are you happy to be alive?

Yes.

Are you happy with Life?

No.

Does that answer your question?

You confuse me.

I feel confused. I am not a seer.

And I trusted you with my life.

We all must take some risks. But you should rather trust a blind man who is confident than a seer who is confused.

But you say you have discovered your Beast. It is Fear. Is that what moves you?

I said each one of us has a Beast to be discovered. It is that which moves this world.

How so? Can it move my limbs now? They feel paralyzed.

The whole world—whatever exists—moves in life. It is Fear that moves everything. Fear of mortality leads to procreation. Fear of hunger leads to cultivation. Fear of poverty leads to industry. Fear of ignorance leads to enlightenment. Fear of evil leads to good. Fear of godlessness leads to God. Fear of Death leads to Life.

How will you conquer this Beast? How can anyone conquer?

When I realize that there is nothing else. There is only my Self. For that alone matters. That consciousness alone is Consciousness. There is nothing else. When I am truly alone, I shall merge with the cosmic Consciousness—*that is when I will kill the Beast. For nothing but I will exist from thereon.*

High hopes. I bet this ganja makes you one with that Cosmic Consciousness.

Ah! Truly. But alas! It is only temporary. That is why the Beast never goes away. But I keep trying. Want to try some? Should I light another chillum?

I'm freezing. I want to urinate.

What is the hesitation? I asked you to meditate on water. You will do better—make water.

Aah! Such a relief.

Many problems in life have simple solutions that people tend to ignore. That is why one needs a guru.

I don't need a guru to teach me to urinate.

At least you are toilet-trained, then.

We are caught here between Life and Death. My mind is restless. I have been rethinking my whole life. I find it funny that such mundane bodily functions still bother and still give release and relief.

What is it? You want to shit now?

You are a gross and disgusting old man. I was talking on another plane. How important are these simple functions, even in this crisis.

Ensnared in metaphysics, you tend to get dismissive of the importance of physical needs. Your being consists of many parts. Your corporeal body is an important part of that being. Think of the body as a chariot. The self is the master. The charioteer is your intellect. The senses are horses. The reins are your mind. When a chariot moves, all are involved equally. Who can tell what is the most important component? But one thing is for sure—the thing will not budge if there is a problem with the chariot itself. In the crisis of life's battlefield, the wheels must continue turning, unnoticed and unconscious. But that doesn't make it any less important.

I think my wheels are getting clogged.

Put some oil in the axle. Have some ganja.

You are incorrigible. I am thirsty.

Then drink your fill. There is certainly enough water around to quench a village.

But I feel queasy.

Why is that?

I just pissed into it.

You are a great disciple—a true seer. What took wise men aeons to unravel, you have understood in a few minutes.

What do you mean? I am really thirsty.

There once was a wise man. His disciples asked him to reveal the nature of the true essence of this world. The master asked his disciples to fetch a saucer of water and some salt. When they did so, he asked them to mix the salt in the water. He asked them to come back the next morning. When the disciples returned the following morning, eager to learn, the master asked them to look for the salt in the saucer. They couldn't find it. Then he asked them to take a sip from that saucer. "How does it taste?" he asked. "Salty," came their reply. "That," the master told his disciples, "is the essence of salt—mixed in water, you can't see it, you can't touch it, yet you can feel its presence in the saucer." Similarly, the essence of life, which is Self, cannot be touched or seen, but it can be perceived. The depth of your wisdom surprises me.

Yeah! So now I know there is piss in this water. Some deep wisdom, that.

You are being modest—otherwise why should you be so queasy? Besides, some sages say your own piss is elixir. If you drink it regularly, you will find everlasting health.

Chchih. I am going to throw up.

Drink some water before you do that, for then there will be puke and piss in this water, and that, I presume, will be too much for your heightened perception.

Aah! At least it doesn't taste like piss.

Amazing! I myself have never tasted my urine.

Shut your filthy mouth up or I will drown you in all this piss here.

Wonderful. You are rediscovering your True Self. For a while you had me worried. Do you feel the warmth now, inside?

I could burn your shriveled body. I think I have a fever.

Now that you are more yourself, quenched and relieved, let us talk of more pleasant things.

Didn't you say that what is pleasant need not necessarily be good?

I didn't—some other shriveled soul like me said it. I just mentioned it to you. And in any case, we are going to talk about your life. I presume that hasn't been too good, so we are on safe ground.

I don't want to talk about my life.

Nevertheless. Or would you prefer I continue with my disgusting thoughts?

My mother loved me.

Mine, too.

Whose story is it going to be?

Sorry. Do go on.

She came from East Bengal just before the '71 war. Her father was a tailor, and they moved across the country till they got here and settled. There were three sisters. My *ammi* was the youngest and prettiest of the three. Her mother died when she was still a child. My grandfather was a holy, God-fearing man. When life became too difficult in East Bengal, he migrated to India with his daughters. The girls helped him in his tailoring job, and they all led a relatively happy existence for a while. Slowly, my aunts got married and moved away, leaving only my *ammi* to look after my aging grandfather. By then my grandfather had bought a small shop in the town, and they lived in a room behind the shop. One day a handsome man came to the shop to get some clothes stitched. He was an ex-army man working as an explosives expert in one of the mines. He saw my *ammi* and soon asked for her hand from my grandfather. My grandfather was happy that my *ammi* would be married to someone who lived in the same town. He agreed, even though the man was much older than my mother. My *ammi* did not want to get married—she didn't want to leave her father alone in his old age. But my grandfather convinced her. He was worried about her fate after his death.

A fruitless exercise, that. No point in worrying about fate.

I shall be silent now.

Oh! Don't. Allow an old man his idiosyncrasies. I am really interested in knowing about your life. In the past, whatever little you've revealed pertains more to the colorful exploits of your phallus than to your history.

There is history in the exploits of my phallus, too.

Well said. There is destiny in the fall of a sparrow as well. But do continue.

You distract me. So I was saying, my grandfather got my *ammi* married to this man who was to become my father. Unfortunately, working with explosives had made him volatile, as my poor *ammi* soon found out. He was moody, ill tempered, and violent. Beatings and lashings became a routine for my mother. But she never complained to my grandfather. She suffered in silence.

To surrender to wrongs is to commit them.

Spare me your homilies. Let me talk. My *ammi* delivered me on a wet rainy night of agony.

Strange. Birth is painful for the giver, unlike life, which is pleasurable to the taker. Perhaps giving is always more painful than taking. Where was your unfortunate father?

He was away at the neighboring town with his other wife. He had four. My *ammi* was the youngest. My father was not happy with my birth—he already had several children, and the burden was too much. He thrashed my mother for weeks, till she promised that she would not ask for his support in bringing me up. She took up stitching clothes and soon became a popular tailor, especially for wedding ensembles. She ran her house and brought me up. My father soon got tired of her piety and uncomplaining devotion. He liked challenges. His time spent with us reduced over the years till eventually, he vanished completely from our lives, leaving my mother to pay the rent, run the house, and rear me all by herself. *Ammi* worked hard and put me in school, but her work left her too little time to supervise me. I grew up in that rough neighborhood, spending long hours in the company of boys who were no good. I, too, resented her piety—I thought it had driven my father away. I had inherited my father's temperament and turned out to be a mean-tempered boy. The more my mother tried to correct me, the worse I became.

The more you blow at the ember, the hotter it grows. The more you tug at a knot, the tighter it becomes.

I started drugs, drank a lot, and gambled. When *Ammi* realized the foul uses I was finding for the money she gave me to spend, she drastically reduced my allowance. In retaliation, I became a petty criminal. I joined the local gang of pickpockets and was put in jail for the first time at the age of fourteen. My mother was heartbroken.

That explains the ease with which you answered the hypothetical question I raised about the robber.

Shut up. Shut up. She paid some bribes and took me home. She tried to talk to me, reason with me, but it was no use. I was too far gone. I fell lower and lower into the marsh of crime. I even started bringing home associates, much against the wishes of my *ammi.* One night when I was under seventeen, I brought home two older men who were part of my gang of thieves. They gave me some money and a packet to be delivered to a pawnbroker in a nearby village. It took me a few hours to accomplish that. I returned to find the door ajar, my guests gone, and my poor *ammi* lying on her bed in a pool of blood and shame. She had been gang-raped. I cannot described what I felt then. I felt like exploding—like one of those devices my father used to work with. My mother calmed me down and made me promise that I would leave the company I'd kept and lead a crime-free life. She also made me promise that I would never take any intoxicants. I gave her my word and wept to sleep at her feet. I woke up in the morning to find that she had slashed her wrists and bled to death. The world became my enemy, and I lost track of time and place for weeks. I went to a *masjid* and spent days there, just staring at the sky, listening to *quawwalis* and *naaths.* I became God-fearing—after what He did to me for not believing. But I remained violent. The *maulvi sahib,* a kind old man, knew someone in these mines, and he got me a job here. And here we are.

A moving tale.

Is that all? I spill my guts out, and all you can say is that it is a moving tale?

We are precariously perched on this tree, remember? Too much movement will topple us. But now I understand why you think your business in life is incomplete.

Yes, there are so many turns I took wrong. I want to retrace my steps and make amends.

You can only aim the bow, but once the arrow has been shot, you cannot change its course. You can never change your past.

I want to shoot a fresh arrow. That is why I want one more chance. I have suffered. I have not known family. I have not known a father's love. I have not known the joy of growing up. I want to raise my own family and give it all that I have missed. That is my only redemption.

When did you realize that?

Just a little while back.

It might be a little too late.

I wish it weren't.

Then it isn't. Believe in Life, and it will claim you. Don't, and Death will subsume you. Think how much you can do if you get out alive.

Yes. There will be so much to do. Wounds to heal. Broken pieces to stick. But that is going to be such a long journey—the very thought wears me down.

Every journey of a million miles must commence with one step.

My legs are tired. They have gone to sleep. I can't walk. I can't move. I am suspended between two worlds—two lives.

Only in the twilight zone is it possible to see the glory of the sun, the moon, and the stars simultaneously. Only in between worlds and in between lives can you know your true self.

But it is so dark here. I am fast losing hope.

Don't. Dwell longer on your memories—they will rekindle hope.

My memories are not that kind. They only evoke despair.

Wrong. They are the only reason you seem to want to continue living. You want to go back to life. Rub the slate clean and write a new story on it.

Yes. I can't hold on much longer.

If that is what you want, you can do it. You have to get back. Here, in between worlds and lives, you stand on a threshold. You can step out just as easily as you can step back in. I suggest you turn right back.

The door has shut. I do not hope to turn.

So all that talk, all those grand professions of love of life, were false. You do not wish to be alive.

That's not true. I want to. More than you can ever imagine. More than I ever suspected. But I see no way.

So you give up?

I don't want to—but I am afraid.

Of what?

Of trying and failing. Afraid that even if I survive, I might be unable to accomplish what I intend to.

In that fear of failure lies success. Discover your Beast now.

My eyes grow heavy. My arms grow weak. My head is melting over my shoulders. I am scared. I am so scared. I feel the shiver creep over me like a predator, stalking my senses, pushing me, making me run. There is no place to run. No place to hide. No legs to run on. No arms to fight back. No eyes to see. No mouth to scream. No teeth to bite. No heart to beat. I am fading away. What is that strange shape? Is that you or some third? A beast or a bird? When I look, there are just the two of us. Then who is that third standing there in the corner, waiting, waiting, waiting?

Don't drift—you are drifting. Hold on. Use your strength. I can feel the level of water falling. You are growing heavier, because I am not growing any weaker. You are sinking. The water must be receding. That is hope.

Tired. So tired. I want to sleep now. Sleep.

Open your eyes. Open them.

You asked me to shut them. Now I can see.

That was then, not now. What do you see? Tell me. Speak to me. Don't sink away.

I see light. Pleasantly white. I see a tunnel breaking through the darkness, boring into light.

That is good. Keep talking. What else is there? What do you see?

The light is white the tunnel is white the end of the tunnel is brightwhite and cool it is so hot here and so cold how can it be both? I feel heavy something is pulling me I am being pulled into that tunnel let me go I want to go if you try to hold me you will lose me if you let me go I will find myself the feelings are returning like birds coming home to roost the wings are tired I want to fold them and lay down I have a long way to go I need strength in my wings the strength is seeping back and I am seeping out toward the tunnel there is light white light at the end of the tunnel it is long and it is getting brighter as I fly should I rest now or continue? What will I find on the other side? The walls are closing in space is getting confined converging to a point of light white light white light the point is getting bigger it is growing into a circle no circles within circles growing growing I gather momentum faster and faster everything is becoming a blur white blur except the point no the circles they are becoming clearer more defined I am reaching it now not too far away not too far now not too far now higher higher swifter swifter swifter and I burst the sky is white the clouds are white the valley below is white the hills around are white the sun is white the stars and the moon also shine they are white who is with me? *Ammi* my own *ammi* stitching a white cloth with white thread smiling a white smile at me *Ammi* I missed you why did you leave me? I have returned and I am white too I have lost color and I have gained white the thread reels out entwines me rolling me up like a bobbin so many twists so many folds I feel dizzy the folds have enwrapped me *Ammi* they are so warm I was so cold I feel safe here I was so scared no fears here I have lost the Beast in the white hole behind and below no other can follow here the Beast was black only white exists here my head has stopped throbbing my eyes have stopped blinking my legs have stopped shivering my chest has stopped heaving my nostrils have stopped flaring my veins have stopped pulsing my ears have stopped aching my stomach has stopped churning my hands have stopped trembling my wings have folded so now let me rest I have arrived arrived arrived.

When did you pass from wakefulness to dreams? When did you move deeper into unconsciousness? When did you pass away? Did we come so far only to be separated? The other bird has flown, leaving the bough lighter, emptier. The leaves are still shaking, but the bird has flown. Why did you follow if you had to fly away? What scared you off? I was there by your side. That was enough. What was the thing that instilled you with fear? What Beast? Did you finally find it, or did it find you? I still feel your cold hands on my knees. How hard they held—how weakly. I felt it when they transformed into wings. I could touch the feathers when you outstretched them to fly. So fast you rose, like an eagle. I couldn't follow. I tried, but your wings were mightier, bigger and younger. I flitted, thrown aside by the great flap of your wings, and fell back. I returned to this branch, and now there is no one else. You have gone too far for my poor wings to follow. I am more earthbound. I could not soar through the tunnel to the higher reaches where you wanted to go. I couldn't hold you back. You wanted to be set free. Are you free now? Contented? Now let me return to my world.

I see you. Crouching in the corner like a thief. Stealer of peace! I know you now. Don't hide there—come forth. Reveal your form. How you have haunted me all these years! How I have hunted you. Now we are here in this time and this place. Come out and let me see you properly. After all these years of togetherness, are you turning shy? Timid?

Don't do that. You will take all the glory away from my fears. Why are you rustling in that corner? Come up to the center of the cave so we can judge who is mightier. You who have spread like a septic wound in my mind should not dither. Let this be our much awaited communion. Let us be one henceforth.

Raimoti, sitting on the narrow ledge, leans over to watch a drenched muskrat wriggle through the fast-receding water. The little beast stops, surprised by this sign of activity in this dead place. They eye each other for a brief moment, gauging the reactions. The muskrat is afraid of the looming creature and worriedly shakes his bedraggled coat, sprinkling Raimoti with a fine spray of water.

Raimoti laughs, taking a long drag on his *chillum*, and leans back against the ceiling. There is a sudden crash, and the ledge crumbles, leaving a gaping hole in the wall.

Raimoti has no time to react, and he tumbles headfirst through the opening, over to the other side. Does it open into Mine Number 2? Through that he goes up—or is it down? Through that he goes to the moon. It opens up like a window, and through that he goes to the sun. It opens up like a gateway. Through that he goes.

The muskrat, relieved, dives back into the draining water with a tiny splash, seeking a safer exit hole from this wretched place.

chapter 8

Pandey*ji* squelches through the slushy water, hastily sidestepping the slimy muskrat scurrying across the field. He silently curses Bibhash for going and dying on him, leaving him to deal with this immense pile of dung. The man was absolutely unreliable. He didn't even arrange for soda. At least Bibhash submitted his first information report before dying. It is good—full of details and insights. Now Pandey*ji* has to wind up here at the site and get back, rehash the damn thing to glorify his own crucial role in handling the entire situation, and submit it as his own. Pandey*ji* is not too sound on the technicalities, and he feels a grudging gratitude toward Bibhash for having done all the groundwork.

Followed by a dozen or so functionaries from the subarea office, Pandey*ji* walks purposefully through the crowd, ignoring the gibes, the suppressed surges of the crowd, to the office building. Someone conducts him to the room designated for the subarea manager—the room occupied by the late Bibhash Mukherjee. Ignoring the *hai-hai* and the even cruder slogan shouting, Pandey*ji* squeezes into the wobbly, uncomfortable swivel chair. He looks around at the depressing, shabby dump that passes as the subarea's office. There are two gray steel *almirahs* against one wall, tilting at a dangerous angle. On the wall facing the chair is a blackboard with some statistics and a large map of the underground, color-coded to show the progress of work in various blocks. There are heaps of dusty khaki files everywhere—above the *almirahs,* on the table, and even, to Pandey*ji*'s disapproval, on the floor. Loose sheets and slips of paper flutter about in the noisy breeze from the wall-mounted fan. There is no personal touch to the office, as if Bibhash didn't want to be associated with his work. The only thing of Bibhash's in the room is a plastic framed photograph showing a pretty but mournful woman and two chubby little girls. Pandey*ji* finds the clutter distracting and removes everything from the tabletop, shoving the photo into the drawer.

Pandey*ji* summons Balwant and Ram Babu to brief him about the disaster. He is brought up to date on the events of the night. Pandey*ji* dwells only briefly on the drowning of Bibhash and is surprised to realize that the subarea manager has suddenly acquired the status of a martyr in the eyes of the workers. He files away the information for future reference. He will have to tackle that—he wants no martyrs here, he wants an already dead sacrificial lamb. When Balwant and Ram Babu are finished, Pandey*ji* sends for the station house officer from the local *thana,* Inspector Singh, who is outside, supervising the pumping and keeping an eye on the mob.

Inspector Singh is a stout, dark person with an obviously fragile ego. He sinks into the visitors' chair and demands some cold water. Pandey*ji* instructs the attending peon to fetch some water, to be followed by tea and some biscuits. It is almost four in the morning, and refreshments will perhaps be welcome, no? Inspector Singh pulls out a packet of Wills Navy Cut, but before he can light one, Pandey*ji* whips out his own pack of Dunhills and a silver-plated Ronson lighter. The two smoke in silence, formulating strategies to tackle each other. The peon arrives with a tray of chilled water, and Singh drinks thirstily. Even Pandey*ji* is thirsty—whiskey always leaves him dry-mouthed.

"So," Pandey*ji* says, clearing his throat, "it must be a pain getting pulled out of bed for something like this."

"Duty. I am used to worse," Singh replies gruffly.

"Oh! I am sure, I am sure," Pandey*ji* agrees, "yours is a tough job, no doubt."

"Made tougher by some others who are far more lax than they can afford to be."

"I know what you mean. That Bibhash Mukherjee was a laggard. He should have reacted with greater speed."

"I don't know what you people were up to, trying to speak to the superintendent of police and the deputy superintendent of police *sahib*. You should have sent someone down to inform me. After all, the SP or the DSP is not on the spot—out here, I am in control."

"Er—I think Bibhash spoke to your lieutenant, the *thana* sub-inspector on duty, and he was told that you were out on a tour."

"Nonsense!" Singh replies angrily. "He couldn't have said that. I was very much in town—at my residence. After all, you don't expect that I spend my entire life at the *thana*, do you?"

Pandey*ji* realizes that he is treading on touchy ground and skillfully changes the line of conversation. "That Bibhash was a fool. Tell me, Singh *sahib,* did you have time to get informed about the incident—I mean, briefed in a manner fit for a senior officer like you?"

"No. From the time I was reached about an hour back, I have been too busy coordinating with the fire brigade and keeping the crowd under control. It is disgusting that none of you senior managers from the company were around. We even have to do *your* job."

"Oh! But I personally sent Mukherjee to supervise the rescue operation and talk to the workers while I reported to the board members. That was of paramount importance, I'm sure you will agree. We are talking about not only the loss of a few lives but also the potential loss of government assets, worth several millions. Delay in such vital information relating to the interest of the nation is not tolerated, as you well understand. In fact," Pandey*ji* adds in hushed tones, "we have an officer from the ministry right here tonight—Mr. Karna—putting up at the guesthouse. Any laxity on our part will be reported immediately to the highest quarters. He was deeply concerned about the delayed response from the police and the fire brigade and wanted to highlight that in his report. When Mukherjee informed us that the police station house officer was untraceable, Karna *sahib* was very agitated and wanted to speak to the home ministry right away. I dissuaded him, knowing how unreliable Mukherjee could be. A good thing I did, I see, now that you tell me all this happened while you were at home."

Pandey*ji*'s bluff seems to have paid off. Singh looks a little shaken. Perhaps, as Pandey*ji* suspects, Singh was absent from his jurisdiction without official permission or intimation. If this fact gets out, the SHO could land in big trouble. The apparent loss of composure on his part betrays the chink in Singh's armor. Pandey*ji,* a past master of such games, presses on a little more confidently than before.

"Of course, Karna *sahib* wanted me to confirm this fact before he spoke to the home ministry. What better confirmation can I get than your word that you were at home? I am sure this Mukherjee had either misunderstood or cooked up some tall tale to cover for his own delay in contacting you. I will put in the right word to Karna *sahib* when I see him later this morning."

"Hmmm. You are right. This Mukherjee fellow was useless. Irresponsible, I say! I can give you many examples of his utter ineptitude in handling crises. I have been in this *thana* for two years, and I know all about Mukherjee's alcoholism and even"—Singh lowers his voice conspiratorially—"his perversions—he collected pirated pornographic videos. I could have raided his room and arrested him anytime. But I took pity on him. He looked so sickly and unmanly—a *hijra.* But what do I get? The bastard goes and makes a false accusation of dereliction of post against me. Had he been alive, I would have fixed him good!"

"*Arre,* Singh *sahib,* forget Mukherjee," Pandey*ji* says dismissively, "that worthless fool. Here, have some hot tea—it's quite chilly in the mornings already, isn't it? Biscuits? So, tell me, has a police report been filed yet?"

"No," Singh says, slurping noisily from his cup. "I have the reader compiling that. We will file it tomorrow—I mean later today."

"Is it possible for me to have a look at the draft before it becomes official? I would like to compare it with mine—to check for any glaring discrepancies, you know."

"What? You are also preparing a report?"

"But of course. I have to—it's mandatory."

"In that case, could you show it to me before I finalize mine?"

"Certainly," Pandey*ji* says cheerfully. "After all, we are different arms of the same entity. We must work in tandem. Our versions must be—ah—properly coordinated."

"Absolutely. We will sit together this afternoon and finalize the reports. You can help me edit out the minor, unnecessary details, and I can help you put everything in the right—what shall I say—perspective."

"Excellent! Now for the business at hand. How is the mood of the crowd?"

"Ominous!" Singh says. "It has taken my personal presence here to keep the mob under control. The workers are extremely agitated. They are saying all sorts of things about the management. They are also accusing you of not having taken sufficient and timely interest in the whole thing. I had to resort to a mild *lathi* charge—a very mild one, mind you, to prevent them from entering and occupying this office building. There is that leftist leader out here, Ghosh, who has been whipping up mass hysteria, exhorting the workers to go on indefinite strike. Well, that is really not my business, these industrial relation matters, but I want no law-and-order situation on my hands. No rioting, no arson."

The rhythmic slogan shouting outside suddenly acquires overtones of a battle cry. It rises in pitch and crescendo, culminating in a mighty roar of victory. This is followed by a loud crash. Pandey*ji* and Singh rush to the window and peek outside from behind the curtains. The crazed mob has tied several thick ropes to the winder tower above the shaft, and they have just managed to pull down the topmost segment of the looming structure. Some of them are dancing in a frenzy, shouting slogans against Pandey*ji*, the company, the government, the police—everything. Pandey*ji* can make out the figure of Ghosh *da* striking a pose near the cage platform. He is swaying like a man possessed and making wild, accusatory gestures toward the office building. Some of the men around him have already started turning in that direction. Many of them have shovels and pickaxes that they are swinging in sync with their furious chant.

"I must call for reinforcements," Singh says hastily, returning to the table and grabbing the phone. "This is turning into an ugly situation. I have only twenty constables with me, and only four are armed, and even those carry nothing more than the relic .410s."

While Singh makes his calls, on both the telephone and the VHF radio handset, Pandey*ji* watches the violent mob outside with fear. The entire seething mass of about five hundred mine workers and family members seems to have transformed into a mindless, wild beast. Pandey*ji* feels his throat go dry as he observes about a score of men starting to walk purposefully toward the office. He looks back. Singh is still engrossed in his calls.

"Singh *sahib*," Pandey*ji* shouts hoarsely, "the crowd is moving toward this office. It looks pretty aggressive. Do something—don't just stand there making calls."

"Don't tell me what I should do. You do your own job and let me do mine. Why don't you go out and try to pacify the workers? After all, that is your responsibility."

"Are you crazy? You want me to go out and face that—that monster now? They will lynch me even before I can start talking to them. I know labor psychology. They can get quite brutal. At this moment they are angry and have to vent it. For them this office is a symbol for the company, and I am the representative. They don't understand that I have nothing to do with all this—that Mukherjee was responsible for everything."

"Then go out and explain that," Singh shouts back. "I am telling you, I don't have the manpower to control them. I have to wait for the reinforcements."

"I can't. I can't. I can't," Pandey*ji* says hysterically. "They will not listen. They are like a pack of wild dogs right now. They will tear me apart without a thought. I need a lure, a bait, to divert their attention. For that I need to talk to my superiors. Now. Please buy me some time—just half an hour and I will have something to tackle them with."

"You want me to go out and face that mob with ten *lathis* and four guns? Are you crazy? Let's lock up from inside and barricade. Wait for the reinforcements."

"That won't do. They will burn down the building. You go out. Talk to them. Order a *lathi* charge—air fire—*anything*. Just keep them at bay for half an hour. Then I will talk to them. They will listen to you—you and your men are in uniform. They fear uniforms. Go now—go. Before it is too late."

Pandey*ji* literally pushes Singh out of the room and bolts the door from inside. He looks around and then barricades the entrance with the four visitors' chairs. He returns to the table and dials the residential number of the director. No response. He tries another number—still no response. His panic rises with the increasing noise outside. Suddenly, he hears a shot. It appears to be from Singh's service revolver. The commotion subsides. He can hear Singh's voice screaming over the roar of the crowd. Pandey*ji* cannot make out a word of it but is relieved that Singh has apparently managed to hold the mob back, if only for a while. Someone picks up the receiver at the other end.

Pandey*ji* is lucky. He has managed to get through to one of the directors. He quickly relates the situation and requests permission to announce some compensation or awards immediately. The director replies that the decision is beyond his purview and that he will have to discuss the matter with the CEO and other directors. Pandey*ji* whines, cajoles, cries, and finally convinces the director to call back with approval for announcement of some interim compensation. The director promises to call back within half an hour.

The next thirty minutes are the longest in Pandey*ji*'s—till now—relatively trouble-free existence. He sits on Bibhash's wobbly chair, drinking water and cursing the dead man. He makes another call to the guesthouse to check on Karna *sahib*. He is relieved to be informed that the VIP is sleeping and there is no sign of any trouble. All is quiet back there.

It is far from quiet outside the office. The crowd, which seemed to have been momentarily taken aback by the forceful presence of Singh, now seems to be redeploying around the building. Pandey*ji* takes a quick peek out the window and sees hundreds of people assembling in the compound. They have completely dismantled the winder tower and gravitated toward the large office compound where Ghosh *da* is holding forth, standing on a table someone has provided him. Singh and his men are huddled on the veranda, looking quite helpless and barely in control. There is no sign of reinforcements.

This is not the first time Inspector Singh has faced a mob, and it is not the first time he's found his mouth dry. The eastern sky is already lighting up, with the predawn glow silhouetting the broken tower. It could have been just another peaceful morning if not for the hundreds of seething miners surrounding him.

Nervously, he pats his ammunition belt and is relieved to find that he has remembered to put a dozen or so bullets in it. He glances at the nearest armed constable. *It is ridiculous how young some of these chaps are,* he thinks. The boy still has a soft down on his upper lip, which is pursed in tension. Singh wonders if the boy has ever shot at human bodies. Probably not. He turns his attention back to the crowd.

Ghosh *da* has stopped his oration and is staring darkly at Singh and his men. A quiet has descended on the scene in front, like a lull before a storm. Singh knows the psychology of these men well. They are a beaten and resigned lot used to being bossed around. Their long and arduous hours below the ground sap their spirit. Individually, they are no better than street dogs that can be kicked around and bullied. Normally, a single constable is enough to quell a drunken brawl or personal quarrel. These are mere laborers with no expectations from the society or fear of the government.

But Singh also knows that united, the same broken men can be violent, fearless and uncontrollable. They carry such explosive pains and sorrows within that a small spark can make them erupt like a volcano, destroying everything that comes in their way. They are desperate men who can take drastic steps when they collide.

Singh narrows his eyes as he silently watches a young miner in his trademark blue uniform edging toward the veranda. The line of cane-wielding constables cordoning the subarea office coils up imperceptibly. Singh can hear early birds at a distance, incongruously chirping in the new dawn. A rooster crows somewhere. Everything is still. Hundreds of bloodshot eyes are watching the young miner, who comes to a defiant stop in the no-man's-land between the mob and the police cordon.

A couple of grimy street dogs race through the intervening space, chasing each other playfully, making the constables nervous. The four armed constables stand gripping their outdated single-shot .410 rifles meant for crowd control. Singh unbuttons his side holster discreetly, freeing his .32 standard-issue revolver for quick draw. His previous fire was more of a formality than a requirement. It convinced no one, not even his own men. He mentally calculates his firepower and grits his teeth. The mob is at a distance of about fifty meters, and with the kind of untrained gunmen he has, the chances of hitting someone are negligible. His own .32 is nothing but a noisy stick at that range. Even if he orders firing—for which he will later be hauled over burning coals by the civilian administration and politicians—they won't be able to hold back the crowd, and the retaliation will be swift and brutal. His cane-wielding men will be even less effective. His options are nonexistent. He has to hope the miners can be psychologically dominated. Only he isn't sure if animals have a psychology. He licks his drying lips and doesn't move.

The young miner looks over his shoulder at the horde of workers behind him. Then he takes another tentative step ahead. He is now barely ten meters from the cordon. A few men give a small cheer, egging him on. They want to test Singh's determination and reactions. On his makeshift dais, Ghosh *da* leans down and whispers something into the ear of one of his cohorts. A miner takes up the large red flag of their labor union and rushes across to hand it to the moment's hero. Singh groans inwardly.

Almost pompously, the young miner grips the bamboo pole and waves the flag in wide arcs. He takes another couple of steps, bringing him dangerously close to Singh's men, who are about as disciplined as a bunch of schoolkids. Any closer, and the miner will be in the striking range of the canes, and then anything can happen. Singh doesn't even want to think about what he will do if one of his men gets too jittery and strikes out. He wants to remain in control as long as he can, or lose control at the right time. He has to do something now. The crowd is getting emboldened, and there is an increased charge of menace in the air. They sense Singh's dilemma and are on the point of seizing the moment.

Singh adjusts his peaked cap and tucks his shirt into the broad leather belt below his flabby belly and forces his body to saunter down the veranda to the shallow flight of steps. He stands there, hands casually placed on his hips, and glares at the advancing man.

His insouciance is cunningly calculated. Ruffled, the man stops uncertainly, with the union flag fluttering limply above him.

"Stand back, everyone," Singh shouts across the compound after an adequate dramatic pause. He hopes that he has been able to keep the tremor out of his voice. "We don't want any trouble here. GM *sahib* is trying to get in touch with the company directors, and we should be hearing from him soon. Please calm down and stand back. We don't want anyone to get hurt."

There is a howl of rage from the crowd, followed by some derisive heckling. Singh stands it out. He notices that the man before him is still indecisive about how much of a hero he wants to be. Singh decides to press on. "We know this is your internal matter." He's trying to sound reasonable, almost friendly, distancing himself and his men. He wants to convey that the police are treating this as mere industrial dispute. "But it is our duty to ensure that no one does anything foolish. I understand your sentiments at this moment but strongly urge you to exercise restraint. We don't want to make any arrests over such a small issue." He tries to play down the seriousness of the situation. The threat of arrest is subtle, designed to lodge itself in the crowd's subconscious.

Ghosh *da* bridles and rises to the challenge in this game of nerves. "Go ahead," he bellows back. "Arrest me. *Arrest us all!*"

Singh lets this counter-challenge hang in the air, seemingly unnoticed. He knows when not to get baited; he says nothing.

The crowd cheers their leader lustily—he has made the policeman speechless. This is what they want. At least sometimes the arrogant bastards in khaki should have their noses rubbed in the ground.

The miner with the flag feels secure again and waves it once more. He takes a few more steps toward the veranda. Now he is well within effective striking range. It is still an impasse. If Singh orders a *lathi* charge, the man will be stopped, but then it will be impossible to deal with the ire of the workers. He has to think of something quickly.

He steps down from the veranda casually, as if strolling down a garden path, and walks over to stand just behind his cordon of men. With his hands clasped behind his back, he paces the line from one end to another, making the miner edgy. Singh concludes that the man is close enough to hear him but far enough from his comrades to prevent them from listening to what is said. He makes up his mind. His long years in the police have taught him to hit where it hurts the most. The momentary hero is the chink he is looking for.

"Look, my friend," Singh says softly, barely moving his lips, "you are just a boy getting carried away in the heat of the moment. But remember, I and my men now recognize your face and won't forget it tomorrow."

He keeps pacing up and down, allowing time for the implications to sink in, enjoying the sound of fine gravel crunching beneath his polished boots. He knows that Ghosh *da* and the crowd must be wondering what's going on. Good. He can also sense the relief of his men, who have quickly grasped what he is trying to do. One of the constables catches Singh's eyes and grins. The inspector smiles back, making sure the crowd can see his face. He could be cracking a friendly joke.

"So," he continues conversationally, "no matter what happens now, we are going to get you tomorrow or the day after. If not you, then someone from your family. You have a mother? Sister? A wife? Oh! My boys will find them. They enjoy women."

Singh stops walking and looks at the young miner, who is no longer waving his flag; he is fast sliding down his heroic pinnacle to the valleys of reality. He is, after all, only a poor worker. Singh's words are a quick reminder of that incontrovertible fact. The miner looks at the ground.

"Moreover," Singh says as he commences pacing once more, "I am ordering my boys to smash your kneecaps and arms now if you move—either toward or away from us. You are safe only while you stand here. You can wave your stupid rag and scream slogans, but you cannot move. You can't go back to your pathetic comrades and complain. Have you seen how a man with smashed kneecaps crawls? *All his life. Han?* Have you seen a man with no arms? How will you wipe your shit, son? Think about it as you stand here. I am returning to the veranda. If you move, my men will know what to do."

Leisurely, he turns on his heels and starts to walk away. Then a thought strikes him, and he halts.

"Oh! And one more thing," Singh says over his shoulder, "if you utter a word of this to anyone, today or later, I will know. So be very careful. Some of my boys like men, too. Want to be a hero, don't you? Now resume your flag waving and slogans before I reach the veranda—I don't want them to suspect anything. If you don't, prepare to crawl all your life."

He walks away with a soft chuckle. He knows he has checkmated the aspiring hero.

The crowd of miners stands across the compound in confused silence. They saw the inspector say things but couldn't hear him. Their brave comrade had stood his ground despite whatever Singh had said to him. But why is the man quiet? Has Singh tried to intimidate him? The miners are getting impatient and angry. They wait to see what Singh is going to do next before reacting.

Ghosh *da* watches the policeman through hooded eyes—what is the fellow up to? Singh pauses a brief moment before reaching the steps to the veranda and glances back. At that moment the young miner lets out a roar. *"Eeeeen-qua-laaab!"* he screams, wildly waving the red flag. *Revolution!*

"Zindabad!" The miners jubilantly take up the age-old war cry of workers. *Long live the revolution.* Ghosh *da*'s brooding face cracks into a wide grin. He doesn't notice the smug twitch on Singh's lips.

The boy has done it. He has shown the police goons the true might of the workers. He has infused the miners with a new sense of defiance. This was a symbolic victory. For a while Ghosh *da* was worried that Singh would do something stupid, like hitting the man with the flag. Then Ghosh *da* would have been expected to lead a retaliatory charge. There was danger of getting caned or shot at. But all is well now. Singh is back on the veranda, neutralized. Ghosh *da* can concentrate on the lesser threat of Pandey.

One of the workers spots Pandey*ji* at the window and points at him with a shout. Ghosh *da* looks up and raises his fist in a regal gesture of *inqualab.* Someone throws a pebble, and Pandey*ji* hastily shuts the window. There follows a hail of stones, bricks, and pebbles picked up from around the compound. The glass panes shatter into bits. A handful of policemen make a symbolic foray into the crowd but immediately retreat onto the relative safety of the veranda, pushed back by the implied violence. It is not their battle after all. Pandey*ji* curses the SHO under his breath and cowers under the table as the brickbats continue. At least the mob can't enter the building, thanks to the presence of the men in khaki.

The phone rings loudly, shaking Pandey*ji* out from under the table. It is the director. He has good news. He says the CEO has approved an interim package for compensation. The modalities of how and to whom the benefits will be awarded will take time to be worked out, but yes, Pandey*ji* can go ahead and announce the news on behalf of the company.

Pandey*ji* carefully jots down the salient points of the package and profusely thanks his director.

The problem he faces now is to communicate with the SHO outside. He wants to take no risks. He first wants the police to announce that the company has declared major compensation to those injured or killed in the disaster. He approaches the window again and parts the faded pink curtains.

"Send the SHO to me!" he screams into the crowd. "Send the SHO to me! I have an announcement to make that will make you happy. Send Singh *sahib* to me!"

There are a few more stones, but someone has the sense to convey the message to the SHO. There is a loud rap on the door.

"Open up! It's me, Singh."

"Is there anyone else with you?"

"No. Just my head constable. Open."

"I want you to talk to Ghosh and tell him that I will announce compensation. Just ask him to come alone. Also ask him to send for one representative each from the families of the five workers who died. Do that and I will open the door. I want you to return with Ghosh."

"Don't give me orders. Open the door now or I will break it down."

"Don't be stupid. I have it. I have the bait. I can handle this from here. Please, I am requesting this as a friend. Do what I say, and you will save both of us a lot of trouble."

A grumbling Singh leaves to talk to the workers. Pandey*ji* watches the scene, crouching below the windowsill, as Singh and three armed constables approach Ghosh's makeshift soapbox. They argue and debate for some time, then, to Pandey*ji*'s immense relief, Ghosh *da* steps down from his dais and walks toward the building. Shortly, there is a knock at the door. "Open up! It's Singh and Ghosh *babu*."

Pandey*ji* drags the chairs away from the door and quickly combs his hair with a pocket comb he always carries. He hand-presses his shirtfront, wipes the sweat away from his forehead, and strides forth to open the door. Ghosh *da* and Singh enter, and Pandey*ji* quickly bolts the door behind them. On Singh's instructions, four policemen stand guard outside. They all take their seats at the table.

"*Namaskar,* Ghosh *da. Aapni kamon aachen?* How is your gout?" Pandey*ji* inquires.

"Do you have something for the workers?" Ghosh *da* asks suspiciously, refusing to get caught up in pleasantries before he is assured that he will have some achievement to boast about to the stupid workers hollering outside.

"Indeed, I do," Pandey*ji* answers proudly, like a magician revealing a trick. "But first, some water? Biscuits? Shall I ask for some tea?"

"Why not? It is nearing my morning tea time, in any case."

Pandey*ji* opens the door a crack and conveys the instructions to one of the local staff standing outside. They sit down, and Pandey*ji* offers his Dunhills around. The peon comes and lays down a tray of biscuits and some tea.

"So, what is the deal?" Ghosh *da* inquires, his voice slightly hoarse from the demagogy.

"Two *lakhs* in cash to the families of the deceased and ten to twenty thousand, depending on the case, to those injured."

"That's all?" Ghosh *da* asks. "What about the others? What about—"

"I am coming to that, Ghosh *da*. Five thousand to each worker who actually went down to attempt a rescue. And last, compensatory employment to one dependent of each of the dead workers."

"You managed this?" Ghosh *da* asks admiringly. "Not bad. Not bad at all."

"I told them that you and your men were threatening to burn down the office and the guesthouse with Karna *sahib* inside, and also set fire to the stockpile of coal waiting to be transported."

"We were?" Ghosh *da* looks adoringly at Pandey*ji*. He loves the man. "And they believed you?"

"I told them they could verify the situation with the local SHO."

"You what?" Singh shouts. "I saw no such attempts!"

"Oh! But we were just going to," Ghosh *da* says cheerfully.

"I also told the director how effectively and efficiently Singh *sahib* has controlled the mob here, almost single-handedly," Pandey*ji* continues smoothly. "The director promised he would see to it that Singh *sahib* gets a commendation, if not a promotion, for this."

Singh is suddenly less resistant to the tenor of the conversation. He knows he did his best—not that there was anything much to do—under the circumstances. But the visions of being commended and perhaps promoted put everything in an entirely different perspective. At once he is with Pandey*ji* and Ghosh *da* in whatever devious intrigue they are plotting.

"Good! Good!" Ghosh *da* says. "But what is in it for me?"

"How is your brother-in-law?" Pandey*ji* asks nonchalantly.

"Still unemployed, even after his diploma in civil engineering. You refuse to give him a job."

"Oh! We didn't have a vacancy earlier. But now—"

"Now?" Ghosh *da* is anxious, hooked.

"Now that we have met, I seem to recall there are a few vacancies in our civil department at the township. I wonder why it never struck me earlier. Do one thing—the first thing after all this dust has settled down—send me the biodata again, and ask your brother-in-law to meet me in my office. I think I might be able to work out something appropriate."

"You know, we are on opposite sides of the table," Ghosh *da* says, taking another Dunhill from Pandey*ji*. "But I really admire your managerial skills. You have handled the situation marvelously tonight. I will certainly mention that to the people in the ministry, where I am due to visit next week. People like you should not be GMs—you should be made a CGM or even a director. You will be an asset to whichever company you join."

"You are too kind. So now, if the relatives of the deceased have arrived, should we talk to them? Will you do the talking, or should I?"

"Oh! Leave that to me. I can handle them better," Ghosh *da* says delightedly. "Besides, I have to speak to the rest of the workers. I must tell them what their spontaneous *inqualab* has achieved. I will tell them they have achieved what few others could in the past—that they have extracted one of the heaviest and speediest compensation packages from the management in the history of this company."

"For that they have only your able leadership to thank, Ghosh *da*," Pandey*ji* quips.

"That is for the workers to decide. They know how to pick diamonds from a coal mine."

"That brings us down to the last pile of garbage to be removed. There is bound to be an inquiry into the disaster. Experts will ask questions. Whenever questions are asked, answers have to be given. One thing leads to another, and suddenly, you are left with more shit on the table than you started with. People will be indicted, decisions condemned. Some of those condemned will start squealing like pigs. Skeletons will emerge from old cupboards. All this will have ramifications, both for you as well as for me or my superiors. No one would want that to happen."

"What are you leading to?" Ghosh *da* asks, puzzled.

"Scapegoat. Punching bag. Call it whatever, but we will be needing one soon."

"You have a suggestion?"

"That would be quite inappropriate, wouldn't it? So let me just think aloud. Bibhash Mukherjee was a recluse—some even say he was a little weird. No one liked him very much. He was a total misfit in his job. As you are aware, he was not in the least popular with the workers—he was always so aloof. A bad attitude for a manager in these mines. He had exceptionally poor public relations. None of his bosses ever had anything to say about him except that he was honest. Ha! That is neither here nor there, is it? In fact, the rumor is, even his wife and kids don't think too highly of him. I hear his wife is having an affair with one of her colleagues from the school where she is teaching. In short, Bibhash was a complete washout. A disaster by himself. No one gives a damn about him."

"Tonight the workers have changed their opinion. He saved Birsa, sacrificing his own life."

"Oh! I've heard all about that," Pandey*ji* says disparagingly. "I believe you were there, and it was only after you made the heroic offer of descending into the pit that he was shamed into going down. Till then he was an object of hate and ridicule among the workers. Correct?"

"True," Ghosh *da* says with a sigh, "but these things change. Workers are simple men. Their perceptions and therefore their opinions change. Once Mukherjee rescued Birsa and died in the process, he became a martyr for us."

"For us?"

"Well," Ghosh *da* says with a shrug, "one has to go along with the masses."

"But I gather that Bibhash committed suicide—is that true? Did you think so, too? I mean, you were there at the time."

"I don't know, really. Mukherjee didn't seem to struggle to save himself. But I really don't know."

"So he could have committed suicide? There is a probability?"

"Yes. But the workers feel otherwise. Don't play with their sentiments. If they want a hero, let them have one."

"Well, we agree that we want a scapegoat. Do you have a better candidate in mind?"

Ghosh *da* is silent.

Pandey*ji* goes on, "Workers are emotional people. Their thoughts are impermanent. You know that. They will remember what you want them to remember, the way you want them to remember. Right?"

"Right."

Ghosh *da* walks out of the room, and Pandey*ji* and Singh sit staring at each other for a long time. Settlement of industrial disputes is a revelation to Singh. Pandey*ji* is a veteran at the game. He is thirsty again and pours out some more chilled water into his glass and sips it, savoring the sweet taste.

chapter 9

Something has to be done about that leaking drainpipe. There is a constant, irritating trickle of drain water that patterns on the corrugated rain-shade through the night, making a racket. The drizzle has subsided. It is a little past five in the morning when Madho knocks on the door. He doesn't have to wait long. This time Tommy opens the door. Dolly is standing just behind, peering anxiously over his shoulder. Madho enters and goes straight to the bathroom to change.

It has been a long, long night, and he is drained. He is keen to wash away the remains of the day that has gone by. He removes his clothes and stands under Dolly's new shower and turns on the tap.

When he reached the subarea office with his friend Prasad, he was hit by an air of gloom among the assembled miners. Those poor laborers were accustomed to deaths and accidents, but each new death was a grim reminder that their turn may come next. The atmosphere was laden with anger. Scores of men and some women were standing around, talking in hushed tones. Some groups were

deep in jingoistic discussions about workers' woes and their even-
tual victory over capitalist exploiters. And inevitably—though it
was barely four in the morning—there were a few men sitting on
the dusty ground in one corner of the compound, drinking dispassionately. What else was there to do?

Madho thought he would see throngs of injured miners and
wailing relatives but was told that Pandey*ji* had arranged a couple
of ambulances for those seriously hurt and requisitioned a few
company jeeps to rush the injured to the nearest hospital, about
twenty-five kilometers away. The skeletal company-run medical
center in Kariakhani has neither the equipment nor the requisite
staff to handle so many cases. Many of the relatives and family
friends were encouraged to accompany them in coal dumpers. Apparently, more than twenty men sustained injuries requiring immediate medical attention, including, of course, the nearly dead
Birsa. The resident company doctor who administered first aid to
the victims and attended to Birsa had changed his mind—later, he
was not very hopeful of the miner's survival.

That probably explained the reduced crowd outside the subarea office, though there was a small cluster of old men, women,
and children huddled near the veranda—relatives of those who
had gotten injured but couldn't go to the hospital for various
reasons.

A few companies of policemen lounged about in one section
of the compound where two troop carriers and half a dozen police
jeeps were parked under a tree. Some of them were standing in
loose groups and smoking *beedis* or chewing tobacco. Madho was
a little surprised by the heavy presence of armed police until some-

one pointed out the torn-down winder tower and told him what had happened. He had missed out on that action.

In a way, it was fortunate for the GM *sahib* that Birsa and Sagan came from distant provinces and lived alone in the mining township. Lakhan and Narasingh were each one of several children of fathers who had worked in the mines for decades and whose families had seen many deaths. Those old mining families had learned to accept the ever looming shadow of death in the mines. Lakhan had two unmarried sisters, and if his death translated into some money that would pay for the girls' dowry, his father would be consoled: he had four other sons. Arif was more feared than liked by most workers and didn't have many friends. Only Raimoti could have caused some trouble for Pandey*ji* over Arif, but . . . And Bibhash was a lost soul for whom no one gave a damn. Luckily for Pandey*ji,* there were no melodramatic relatives beating their breasts and wailing. That could have whipped up passions that would have spilled over and caused some bother for him.

Madho felt like some minor celebrity when he reached the subarea office. People made way for him respectfully, and there was a lot of subdued chatter in his wake. Some came up and offered condolences, while others watched him from a distance, not knowing what to say to a man who has just lost a brother whose body couldn't be found. Somehow men are more impressed and awed by death than by birth, as if the former is a rarer occurrence that happens only to others.

Madho was ushered into a small anteroom where he met representatives of some of the other miners who had died. They nodded at one another and waited in sepulchral silence to be called in to meet the GM *sahib*. They had no need to talk. The following discussions and negotiations left Madho a little dazed. Had it not been for Ghosh *da,* he is sure, he would have accepted much lower terms from Pandey*ji*. Today Ghosh *da* proved why he is so well liked and powerful.

It's his brother who has died, but as Madho washes the suds off under the shower, he feels as if a phase in his life has come to an end.

He comes out dressed in clean *kurta* pajamas and sits down on the sofa. No one speaks for a long time. Madho knows that Dolly is dying of curiosity. He wants to build up the suspense before he relates the news. He notices from the level in the bottle that after his departure, mother and son have been enjoying a few drinks together. Maybe his wife guesses that Madho has returned with good tidings. She has uncanny intuition.

Dolly doesn't want to push Madho at this juncture. Her heart tells her that something good is going to come. Life has rarely dealt her lucky cards; her natural gumption and intuitive flair for taking chances have gotten her what she wants. Her ability to make the right choices at the right time is the only thing that has stood between her and suffering. But today she feels that a windfall is around the corner. Finally, life is going to deal her an ace that she didn't expect.

She allows Madho to believe that, like most women, she is dim-witted and myopic. It is better to keep her husband thinking that she is emotional and too caught up in herself to notice others. It puts him off guard. But the fact is that Madho is the one whose mind she can read like a printed sheet of paper. For all his pretensions, he is simple, transparent, and easy to manipulate. Sometimes so easily that it takes away half the fun for Dolly.

Right now Dolly has seen the gleam in her husband's blood-shot eyes and the small twitch at the corners of his mouth as he tries to suppress a smile. She also notices that he has applied her talcum powder and come out wearing a freshly ironed set of *kurta* pajamas and not his regular night baggies and vest. These are sure signs that he is going to make a special announcement that he expects will please Dolly. And under the circumstances, there is only one thing that he can be so excited about: the company must have declared lucrative compensation for the families of the deceased workers.

Dolly is convinced that if the news had related to the survival of Raimoti, Madho would have announced it on entering. Similarly, had he been disappointed by the company's deal, he would have entered the house in a foul mood, expletives pouring from his mouth. But he did neither. There is only one possible explanation, and Dolly is indeed anxious to hear it. At the same time, she wants to enjoy playing with Madho and test how long he can hold on to the news that he is dying to tell. Any moment now, Dolly feels.

Quietly, Madho pours out a measure of drink for himself and fills the other two glasses on the table. "Cheers!" he says, taking a sip.

Dolly and Tommy raise their own glasses reflexively. "Cheers!" Dolly responds with a mystified smile. "So? What happened?"

"They have confirmed it. Raimoti is officially dead."

"Really? Have they found the body?"

"No. Like I said, that might take some time, even days. But

they sent a team of firemen down to Level Three who came back with the report that water is receding from that level but that Levels Two and One are completely flooded. They say there is no chance that anyone trapped on those levels could have survived—unless . . ."

"Unless?"

"Unless someone is lucky enough to be trapped in an air pocket."

"Air pocket? What's that?"

"When a mine gets flooded so suddenly," Madho explains, "sometimes massive air bubbles are formed near the ceilings, which are higher than other sections of a tunnel. Water rushes in with such force and speed that it pushes air out of the underground. Some of this escaping air gets trapped inside to form air pockets. These pockets can hold enough air to sustain a man or a few men for a long time, even up to two or three days. If Raimoti or any of that gang are fortunate enough to have found such an air pocket, there is a slight chance they might survive till the water level goes down sufficiently to allow a team of divers to locate them."

"Divers? Does the company have divers?"

"No, but they have apparently called for divers from the navy who should get here late this afternoon."

"But," Dolly says agitatedly, "that means it is *still* not certain that Raimoti is dead. He could have found one of those air pockets. That is exactly the sort of thing he would do, if only to spite us."

"Don't be silly," Madho says curtly. "You can't find an air

pocket—you just stumble upon it. There is no predetermined location for these things. It depends on your luck."

"Then I'm sure luck will favor Raimoti. He's that kind. Luck would favor him."

"Yeah? Like of all the forty-eight miners working underground, it was his luck to be with the gang who faced the brunt of the water burst?"

"But suppose Raimoti has found an air pocket. He will survive, won't he?"

"It is not so simple. Even if someone is trapped in an air pocket, the volume of air might be too small to sustain him for very long. Then again, if there are no footholds or ledges where he can rest, he will drown from sheer exhaustion. After all, how long can one keep swimming in a black hole? Raimoti is—was—old. Under such conditions, even a young man in the prime of health would succumb to unnamed fears and claustrophobia. Finally, when the water level starts to fall, it acts like a massive valve, sucking out the remaining air behind it, creating a vacuum that could be so strong that the thinner walls or partitions of such underground chambers could simply implode, collapsing on the survivors. There are odds that my brother could have survived, at least till now, but the odds are *very* uneven and against him."

"Huh! So you think. I will be certain only when the divers show me his corpse."

"How morbid and cruel can you get, Dolly*ji*?" Madho exclaims, shaking his head. "You are talking about my brother, for heaven's sake! In his life, you had no good wishes for him. At least respect his death! Respect the fact that a human being has died."

"Oh! I will respect his death. I will respect him—and love him, too—but only if I am convinced that he will not be coming back to haunt us."

"Even if he becomes a ghost, I'm sure he will never want to haunt you!"

"And what do you mean by that?" Dolly demands. "That I am a *chudail*? A witch? That even a ghost will avoid me?"

"All I meant," Madho replies tiredly, "is that Raimoti's ghost would have no interest in haunting you—it would rather hang from that old *neem* tree near the *dargah*. You don't have to worry about that."

"Well, it better. Or else I will show him what it takes to mess around with me!"

"Aw, Mama," Tommy butts in, getting quite impatient with the discussion, "the old loony is dead. Forget him. Don't you want to ask Daddy*ji* about the discussion with the management? Tell us Daddy*ji*!"

It irks Madho to be addressed like this. Tommy is a good-for-nothing, presumptuous rascal who can get quite tiring. But marrying Dolly was a package deal, just as for Dolly, marrying him was a package deal, including his children and Raimoti. He has tried to encourage Tommy to continue his studies after higher secondary, to get a technical diploma or undertake a vocational course, but Tommy is not interested. He is used to the easy money Dolly has been providing for his nefarious needs. For Dolly, her son is the epitome of masculinity, and she reinforces every expression of his misplaced and often irritating machismo. So if Tommy gets into a brawl, she admires his bravery. If he gets into bed with someone, she adores his virility. And Tommy does both with infuriating frequency.

"Yes, Madho," Dolly echoes, "tell us."

"As you know, I went to the office to meet the GM *sahib*. There was a great crowd outside when I arrived. They called one member from the family of each worker who died in today's disaster. The crowd was restless; there was a large contingent of armed police. Ghosh *da,* from the union, was in consultation with the GM, Pandey*ji*. We had to wait awhile before we were called inside the office to meet Pandey*ji*. Lakhan's old father and Narasingh's eldest brother, Ghosh *da,* Pandey*ji,* and I sat around a table, and we talked about the tragedy. Pandey*ji* expressed his condolences on behalf of the company and asked us how we were related to the deceased. Ghosh *da* was quite vociferous in his criticism of the company policies on safety, promotions, and postings. In fact, he was so aggressive that for a moment I thought Pandey*ji* would throw us all out of the room. But he appears to be a sensitive, understanding man. He readily accepted the blame on behalf of the management and apologized for the failures of Mukherjee, the subarea manager. Ghosh *da* was furious. He told us how unresponsive and inefficient Mukherjee was right through the whole incident.

"You see, it was only after Ghosh *da*—who is not a young man himself—tried to go down to rescue Birsa that Mukherjee was shamed into going down. Mukherjee, as we discovered, didn't even bother to inform the police in time. Then he went back to hide in the guesthouse, and Ghosh *da* had to drag him back. We were quite appalled, hearing about the callousness of that man. Pandey*ji* was very disturbed when he heard about how Mukherjee had conducted himself and sincerely apologized on Mukherjee's behalf. Ghosh *da* wanted the company to withhold all the posthumous benefits due to Mukherjee's family, but Pandey*ji* pleaded that the poor family shouldn't pay for the sins of the officer. Finally, after a great debate, Ghosh *da* relented. But he insisted that in the inquiry, the crucial lapses on Mukherjee's part must not be glossed over. He insisted that the blame must squarely lie on Mukherjee, so that everyone knows who was responsible for the mess. Even though Mukherjee is dead, Ghosh *da* wanted to ensure that the inquiry committee be clear in their verdict against him. That, he said, would be the only retribution for the workers."

"But," Dolly says, "I thought this Mukherjee actually gave up his life trying to save Birsa."

"Oh! That was what *we* initially felt—that Mukherjee was a martyr. But Ghosh *da* and several other workers later revealed that Mukherjee committed suicide: he was apparently so ashamed of his inefficiency and mistakes that he decided to end his life rather than face the humiliation of an inquiry. He never was one to face consequences boldly—everyone knows it. Even in the end, he chose to run away from the inevitable blame that would have come his way. Mukherjee was such a coward."

"Anyway, what about the compensation? Was anything decided?"

"Oh! Yes. Ghosh *da* haggled, and *how*! Pandey*ji* tried to palm off some token doles—twenty-five thousand for the families of those dead and ten for those injured. But Ghosh *da* was a *lion*! He roared and screamed and demanded more. At first Pandey*ji* was extremely reluctant, but when he realized that Ghosh *da* would not let him or the company get away with the measly doles, he went back to his room and called up the CMD. Then he called in Ghosh *da,* and we could all hear our leader really blast the poor CMD, who must have been on the defensive after hearing about Mukherjee.

"Finally, Pandey*ji* and Ghosh *da* emerged, and Ghosh *da* declared victory for us workers over the management. When I heard what Ghosh *da* had managed to wrangle out of the company, I was stunned. So was everyone else. We didn't expect it!"

"What? What?" mother and son ask together, their eyes shining in anticipation.

"Two *lakh* for us as immediate compensation!"

Tommy stares for a moment and then breaks into an impromptu dance, hugging his mother and jumping all over the place, whooping with joy. The commotion brings a bleary-eyed Mona out of the other room. Tommy tells her the good news and embraces her with ardor. Madho doesn't like these gestures of intimacy between Tommy and his favorite daughter, but Dolly tells him it's good for family bonding. Mona is also overjoyed with the news and joins Tommy in the jig. Dolly looks on indulgently.

"This," Madho says, the spirit of celebration catching up, "this is not all!" Everyone freezes. "There is more," Madho continues, relishing every word. "The company has also promised compensatory employment for one member of the affected family. So that means Tommy will get a job. I am sure that if I try, I can get him something good with the help of Ghosh *da.* How's that?"

The reaction to that is mixed. This time Dolly jumps up and gives Madho a warm hug; he almost manages to blush under his black skin. Tommy is less enthusiastic. He is against the very idea of working for a living. He thinks of himself as the crown of creation, and he cannot accept the thought that God ever intended making that crown *work* to earn bread. Besides, Tommy is as well placed as he will ever be. He gets all the money he wants to sustain his lifestyle from his mother, he has a roof over his head, and he has a captive partner in the house for expressing his libido.

"I don't want to work in some wretched mine," Tommy says sulkily.

"But Tommy," Dolly reasons, "it is such a wonderful opportunity! We have been worrying about your job for some time now. Your daddy has talked to so many people, but nothing seemed to be working out. Raimoti's timely death has solved this problem. Aren't you happy? Getting a job isn't easy, you know."

"I don't want to work in a *mine*!" Tommy retorts sullenly.

"Then you should have listened to me and finished college or at least gotten a diploma or something of that sort. What do you think, we will support you all your life?" Madho says with anger.

"Oh! Does that bother you?" Dolly asks archly. "You never seemed so bothered about the prospect of supporting Raimoti for the rest of *his* life."

"Raimoti didn't need to be supported," Madho says. "He supported me through my childhood and youth."

"Well, you don't have to support Tommy—no, you don't. I am there for him," says Dolly, her voice turning brittle and icy.

"I—I didn't mean it that way. You know it, Dolly*ji*," Madho wheedles, hastily backing off. "But shouldn't a man his age be doing something more constructive than *chokribazi* and *gunda-gardi*? He wastes all his time chasing girls and causing trouble with his ruffian friends."

"How old is he? He is just a boy, my poor Tommy—boys will do such things."

"Dolly*ji*, Tommy is eighteen. At his age, I was bringing home a regular income from a regular job."

"You didn't have a *working* and *earning* mother." Dolly's voice is now shaking with anger. How dare Madho forget that she is contributing as much if not more toward the household? Moreover, unlike him, she had to pay a heavy price for getting her job. That last night with Dr. Sen stabs her thoughts like a knife. Memories of all other betrayals and losses come hurtling at her. Fury at her father who abandoned her, the pain of her orphaned childhood, the recollection of the pious weight of Dr. Menon pounding her adolescent body all attack her like a pack of hungry wolves, making her hurt so much. She wants to hurt someone back. "You had a crazy grandfather and an even crazier older brother. Sometimes I think you are no saner. What options did you have, you pathetic wimp?"

Madho is taken aback with the burning anger and hate in his wife's shrill voice. He was only trying to reason with her about Tommy's future. He feels hurt and humiliated. *Why do I take this shit from the bitch?* he wonders, and then despises himself even more because he does not find an explanation. They say that men carry burdens of previous *janma*—past lives—on their soul. Maybe he tortured Dolly in some previous birth and it is his karma to suffer her helplessly in this one?

"If you feel that way, I don't understand why you made all that fuss about getting Tommy a job," he says limply.

"I want a job for him. Not a laborer's job, a respectable office job," Dolly says, regaining control and negotiating. Now is the time for it. She wants to push Madho into making a commitment.

"So? I didn't say I would make him a *mazdoor*. If I get the right contacts, I will get him a decent job in the regional headquarters or maybe even in the company headquarters," Madho offers placatingly.

"So find some contact. That's the least you can do now that Raimoti has saved you the trouble of negotiating with the management."

"That's not so easy."

"Huh," Dolly grunts, "*nothing* is easy for you. Sometimes not even getting it up!" Tommy sniggers, and Mona tries to hide a naughty grin. Her stepmom is something, she thinks, admiring Dolly's onslaught. "If you can't find any contacts in the right places, tell me. You know how good I am at making contacts, no?"

"I'll do something. Don't worry." Madho is furious and glares down Tommy. He knows what his wife is implying. He knows that she still has some old admirers. He has found out that many times when she gives the excuse of "emergency night shift," it is not the company's medical center she goes to. And he knows that she knows he knows, and she always throws it in his face as if it's something to be proud of. It makes Madho mad and want to hit her. But he can't. He sulks glumly.

"Oh, Mama, let's forget this silly matter. I will think about it.

But two *lakhs* is a good sum. I have no problem about that," says Tommy.

"Yes, now we can buy the house that we have been dreaming of. Right, *mera buddhu* Madho? My *jaanu*—sweetheart!" Dolly knows how to work her magic. One loving word, and a sulking Madho turns into a fawning Madho.

"That's right. It is a big relief. I will go to the bank tomorrow." Madho is vastly relieved that Dolly has decided to take off the thumbscrews. Sometimes he overreacts and forgets that, after all, she is a woman, and women are such weak and emotional creatures, especially about their sons. He understands her now that he has calmed down. Of course she loves him. Who else cares for her as much? He decides to change the mood in the house. A man must carry his family on his shoulders. "Come on, Tommy, big boy, pour out another drink, even for Mona! We will toast to that. Where is Tina?"

"Sleeping or weeping, I'm sure," Dolly says with sarcasm. "Trust her to throw a wet blanket on everyone's celebration. Forget her—let's have some fun!"

The happy family drinks a round of rum, then another and another. Tommy puts on a cassette of recent hits on his mother's stereo, and they all celebrate till well after daybreak. Madho gets quite drunk and drags Dolly into their bedroom and locks the door behind them. He is eager to make up with Dolly and knows only one way to do it. Tommy and Mona collapse behind the sofa and soon pass out in a stupor. The house falls silent.

Tina sits alone in the quiet room. Her tears have dried up. She is beyond grief now. She heard the jubilation, the celebration, the bonhomie, in the house, but didn't react. Nothing matters at this stage. Her *kaku* is gone. Dead. She will never see that bony, gnarled, ugly man again. She will never hear his rasping, warm voice as it soars up to meet the skies in search of his God. She will not hear the grim tales of his imagined encounters with his Beast, either. Raimoti is gone from their lives, leaving only some cash and uncontainable joy for his family. He died as he lived—uncared for and giving.

What was the purpose of such an existence? Why did He create such a man, whom no one seems to have wanted, no one seems to have tolerated? Well, that is not true. Tina cared for him. More than she did for anyone else in her young life. She remembers how Raimoti held her little hands, guiding her fingers over the keyboard of the battered old harmonium. She remembers how his voice held hers in a warm and tender embrace as it helped her through the rugged terrain of music. She remembers when he took her to the *neem* tree and spoke about things that no one else seemed to comprehend, but which so many of Tulsi Baba's devotees seemed to cherish. She remembers how he taught her to tend to his *tulsi* shrubs and explained to her the mysteries of the herb. She remembers how he always moved about in a trance, unnoticed and unnoticing, following a hidden, divine beacon. She remembers all this and much more, and she mourns.

She mourns in agony as a friend mourns her companion's death. She mourns in misery as a disciple mourns her master's death. She mourns in anger as a sister mourns her brother's death. She mourns in pity as a mother mourns her infant's death. She mourns in silence as a daughter mourns her father's death. She mourns in desperation as a devotee mourns her god's death. She mourns, weeps, and then weeps some more. Her tears have washed away the grime of derision from Raimoti's harmonium. She covers it with a clean white sheet—a shroud—and lies down next to it. Soon her eyes close and sleep moves in, draping the thorns of her thoughts in a cushion of oblivion. She sleeps.

How quiet and beautiful it is at this time of day. It's still early for full winter, but the air is crisp and cold. The slight mist swirls like rivulets around the still landscape. It will be a few more hours before the struggling autumn sun can push it aside. There is no one at Pir Baba's dargah today—they know that Tulsi Baba has gone. How lovely the neem tree looks, its mighty branches waving tenderly in the breeze: inviting, seeking. The ground is frostybrown, accepting no footprints, offering no dust. Even the dogs are silent, spellbound. Blades of dew-laden wild grass stand, their heads bowed in obeisance to their empress, Tulsi. How regal, how stately, how fragrant, how divine. Is she mourning? Why is she drooped in suffering? There is nothing to worry about. There is someone else who will tend to you, O empress. Someone else will love you, pamper you, worship you. Life goes on. No one is irreplaceable. Life is everywhere, forever replacing, replenishing, and reproducing. But don't forget old friends. After passing through so many doors and windows, there is this last one. Going in is coming out. One last peek into the house of hate and neglect. What? Asleep? All asleep in ecstasy? Dead to the glory of the morning moon? Ah! There you are, beloved, faithful friend! Who has draped you against the chilly breeze? Who has wiped you clean? Will you come? Your place is not here among uncaring souls. You are the staircase to heaven. You are the vehicle of paeans sung to gods. Come. It's time to go. And you, little one? What ails your heart? What pains your mind? Believe in life. Life is irrepressible. Adieu! Forgive the sins of others. Forgive deceit and deception. There is a higher cause than mere existence. Believe in yourself and remember there is one who loves you—for what you are and what you can be. Adieu! Farewell, sweet child!

Tina wakes up with a start. She feels a sudden zephyr of cool, fragrant morning air caress her, reviving her, comforting her. She looks across to where the white sheet lies in a rumpled heap. The harmonium is gone. Tina looks out of the window at the misty world with bleary eyes. It looks wonderful, elevating, magical. The universe is full of possibilities. Death does not always end life. Sometimes it just transforms. Drops of accumulated rainwater fall into the tiny puddle on the windowsill. *Drip! Drip! Drip!* Tina smiles and goes back to sleep.

epilogue

The soft murmur of the artificial waterfall provides a soothing backdrop for the hum of subdued conversation and the clinks of cutlery and chinaware. Atul Karna loves the club. It has the subtle ambience of tradition and sophistication that he finds extremely fulfilling. It calms him just to know that he shares his membership with the one thousand elite of the city. He comes here often, alone or in the company of friends, rich businessmen and rising executives who have far more money but no membership. His guests are invariably impressed and envious. Atul loves it.

This afternoon Atul is here for a luncheon with a senior executive from the UN. They discuss the status of the UN-sponsored foreign training program, which Atul has applied and lobbied for. His guest is very positive—over the months of lobbying, Atul and he have become very friendly and informal. It appears that finally, the application has reached Geneva, and the approval for the two-year fully sponsored course in Brussels is expected within the week.

It puts Atul in a fine mood. He signs the charge slip and escorts his guest to the parking lot. They part with a promise to meet over the weekend for a combined family excursion to a friend's opulent stud farm in the suburbs.

Atul is delighted and calls Rhea, his exquisite wife, on the cell phone. Rhea is thrilled with the news and extracts the promise of dinner at their favorite Thai restaurant this evening. She says she will finish her presentation for the multinational client early and rush back home to change. After packing the kids off to her cousin's, she will meet him directly at the restaurant. Atul confirms the plan and hangs up, cruising off in his shiny new Ford Ikon with a contented smile.

It has taken him months to swing the foreign training, but all the hectic lobbying and lunch and dinner diplomacy have finally paid off. Rhea is already shopping for their two-year sojourn in Europe. They have been through some rough times, especially when Atul was posted in that godforsaken town for three years. Rhea had to continue in the city because she couldn't afford a break in her career at that stage. But now it is different. She has a lot of experience, and she can easily find a job, even if it has to be a part-time consultancy, at any of the top ad agencies in Brussels. Besides, they have saved enough to see them through their stay, even only on his stipend. The change will do them good, and the kids will really benefit from the exposure. Atul can't wait for the letter of nomination from Geneva.

But in the meantime, he thinks morosely, the business of governance must go on. All the file pushing and paper blackening must continue till he receives his relieving orders. The job can be quite depressing. At times he feels he is in a pilotless plane, careening through the skies without direction or destination, while the passengers, oblivious and unconcerned, are busy watching the in-flight movie, doing their own thing, and the crew goes about serving coffee and refreshments without batting an eyelid. It's business as usual. No one is really concerned about the fate of the plane. Some who can occasionally grab a parachute and jump off to safety. The others continue regardless. At least Atul has found himself a parachute.

Working in the government has its own rewards. The contacts, the status, the ability to get your work done, it all comes with the job. True, the pay isn't anything to boast about—Rhea brings home five times as much—but there are things that money alone cannot buy, especially in this country. Atul is happy that Rhea is in the private sector, since they have the best of both worlds. He is not a man of great principles—only the seriously intellectually challenged are, in today's world—but he doesn't like to get his hands dirty. The result is that he has acquired the reputation of being fairly clean, a fact that has shut some doors but opened some others. On the whole, he is pleased with the way things are.

On an intellectual level, government has afforded him fantastic insight into the mechanics of this immense democracy. It has shown him how the nation lives, toils, earns, builds, corrupts, and survives. All this from the comfort of a ringside seat where he doesn't have to personally enter the arena to enjoy the battles. He can sit there, comment, observe, examine, and make suggestions on how the gladiators should train, fight, react, and conduct themselves so they are not killed or maimed. No gladiators mean no spectacle and no spectators. That would be quite improper. The show must go on.

Atul enters his gloomy, musty office and slips effortlessly into his role. His extremely discerning and finicky superiors consider him a dynamic and outstanding officer. He buzzes his section on the intercom and speaks to his subordinate officer. *"Han, Sharmaji?"*

"Yes sir? You are back early, sir. Any good news?"

Atul is popular with his staff. He never pushes too hard and doesn't give too much rein, either. He is just right and informal. Sharma*ji* knows about Brussels and is a well-wisher.

"Nothing as yet. But by the end of next week, perhaps."

"Sir, I have made a wish in the Hanuman temple. If you get the approval, you will have to come with me to offer some *laddoos*."

"Oh? Thank you. I most certainly will. One must appease all the powers that be, right? By the way, what happened to that draft reply to the unstarred parliament question on the Kariakhani disaster?"

"Yes sir, yes sir. It is ready, sir. We got a fax from the company, and we have prepared the draft along the lines you suggested, sir."

"Good, good! Can I see it, please, before you put it in the file?"

"Sure, sir. You can access the shared file folder on your PC and see the draft, sir. The file name is PQ 2014, sir. If you find it okay, sir, I will take a printout and put it in the file, sir."

"Great, great. Incidentally, Sharma*ji*, your tour program to Guwahati has been approved. Hope you enjoy the break!"

"Thank you, sir," Sharma*ji* says, and hangs up.

Atul turns the computer monitor toward him and clicks through the menu to the document. It is in the final format: *Will the minister . . . be pleased to state . . . etc., etc.* Ah! The query and the reply:

a) *Is it true that there was a major disaster in the Kari-akhani coal mines in November last year, where six people, including an engineer, died in the flooding and a seventh succumbed to injuries later?*
   Ans.: Yes sir.

b) *How many such incidents have occurred in various coal mines, and what is the number of lives lost and persons injured in each of these cases since 1973?*
   Ans.: The statement giving the requisite details is placed before the house at annexure A.

c) *Has the government made any efforts to inquire into the causes of the disaster?*
   Ans.: Yes sir. A high-powered multidisciplinary tripartite technical committee (HPMDTTC) has been appointed by this ministry to inquire into the causes of the disaster and submit a detailed report within six months.

d) If yes, has any evidence of negligence on part of the management of the company come to the notice of the government?

e) If so, has the government fixed the responsibility on the concerned officials?

Ans. d) and e): In view of reply at c) above, the question does not arise.

Atul Karna reads the draft with satisfaction. Under his able supervision, the section is getting better with its drafts. He buzzes Sharma*ji* and asks him to submit the draft reply on file. He is certain that it will be approved without any changes. After all, he is an authority on the Kariakhani disaster in the ministry—he is on the HPMDTTC and has submitted a 278-page preliminary report on the subject, thanks to generous input from Pandey*ji*.

The day's most crucial work done, Atul reclines in his high-backed chair and riffles through the stack of CDs he keeps in his drawer. Soft instrumental background music helps him plod through the grim files on his desk. Atul searches and finds the CD he is looking for: Hari Coomar's excellent rendition of evening ragas on *jal-tarang*, "The Sound of Water" live at Royal Albert Hall, London. Atul Karna inserts the CD into the PC, clicks the play tab, and closes his eyes in contentment.

acknowledgments

It's said that a first novel is the most difficult to write. *The Sound of Water* couldn't have been conceived and completed without the encouragement of my family and friends who believed in it. I am grateful to all those who made this book possible: my wife, Shampa, who bore the first brunt of every chapter with patience; Param Jit Mann, who helped mold my thoughts; Subhrajit and Sapna Kar, who focused on making my life easier as a writer.

I benefited from the valuable suggestions of my sister, Sangeeta, who scrutinized the first manuscript with great care. My mother, Bimla Bahadur, and family elders sensibly blessed my endeavor without reading it, but then all blessings matter. I must also thank my children, Tvesha and Nishmanya, and niece, Shardooli, who believe that this is the best book ever written—after the Harry Potter series, of course.

I thank my old friend Anupa Mehta, whose help and guidance were invaluable. I also thank Sunil Gautam and his colleagues at Hanmer MS & L Communications Pvt. Ltd. for their strategic initiatives. Nilima Mansukhani, Bhawani Singh, Sushil Kumar, Sujoy Ghosh, Ritu Chaudhry, and Sumit and Vandita

Saran deserve a special mention for their energetic support.

Yfat Reiss Gendell, my literary agent, and her brilliant team from Foundry Literary Media in New York really impressed me with their sincerity and professionalism. Yfat's enthusiasm about *The Sound of Water* probably exceeds my own. I am also grateful to my Atria editor, Amy Tannenbaum, for her patient understanding and insight. I am fortunate to have the confidence of my American publisher, Judith Curr. I thank her and her team, including Peter Borland, for their faith in my writing.

I am deeply indebted to the executives and workers of Coal India Ltd. and its subsidiaries, particularly Partho Bhattacharya, C. H. Khisty, G. D. Gulab, S. A. Yusuf, and Ajay Kumar, who facilitated my on-site research on coal mining and miners. My batch mates and friends from Hill Grange School, Elphinstone College, the IRS, and other Indian civil services are too many to name here, but I sincerely thank them all for their overwhelming support.

Chapter 7 draws upon thoughts from the Vedas and some of the principal Upanishads, while works of William Blake, Alfred Tennyson, W. B. Yeats, T. S. Eliot, and J.R.R. Tolkien influenced my passages featuring Bibhash. I have borrowed lines from the *ghazal* *"Ranjish hi sahi,"* the song "Comfortably Numb" by Pink Floyd, and the title song from the movie *Mast*. I wish to acknowledge these influences.

Finally, I express my sincere appreciation for the Man Asian Literary Prize, which has created a great platform for unpublished Asian writers.

glossary of local terms

annexure   A term used in the Indian parliament to mean "appendix."

Antakshari   Literally, "with the last syllable." A uniquely Indian television game show wherein various age groups—including children—and teams of celebrity guests compete by singing popular songs, generally from Hindi-language movies. One group begins by singing the opening lines of a song; the opposing group must sing a song starting with the last syllable of the previous song.

ardhangini   Literally, "half of the male's being." Also a term for "wife," because Vedic philosophy believes that the male and female cohabit/coexist to make a whole being.

Arre, kuttey   Literally, "hey, dog."

Arre saala   Equivalent of "damn bugger."

Arrey bhai   "Hey, brother." An exclamatory term.

babu   A term of respect. A suffix to names. Something like *san* in Japanese.

badli **worker**   A temporary worker who may be fired at will.

Bajaj Chetak   A scooter made by Bajaj, the fourth-largest producer of two-wheelers in the world.

besharam   Shameless.

beta   Son.

beti-chod   Daughter fucker.

Bhagwan   God.

bhaiyya   Brother.

Bhajans   Hindu devotional songs.

bhang   Cannabis.

biryani   A rice and meat dish.

bhencho   A variation of *bahin-chod*.

boka choda   Bengali for "dumb fuck."

Bus   Literally, "Is that all?"

Chalo, bahin-chodon   Come on, sister fuckers.

chaupal   Platform around a tree where village folk assemble.

chillum   A *chillum,* or *chilam,* is a pipe used by Indian sadhus (holy men), Rastafarians, and many recreational drug users to smoke cannabis, opium, tobacco, etc. The chillum is a conical pipe usually made out of clay, cow's horn, glass, stone, or wood.

chokribazi Womanizing.

chudail An evil witch.

cirag Lamp or light.

dada The complete form of *da*. Literally, "elder brother."

daffli A handheld disk-shaped percussion instrument.

dargah Mausoleum of a Sufi (or Muslim) saint.

Dhat An exclamation of ridicule.

dhowrah A coal-mine slum or shantytown.

durbaan Doorman.

gaand Buttocks; British "arse."

ganja Any of various preparations of different parts of the hemp plant that are smoked, chewed, sniffed, or drunk for their intoxicating or hallucinogenic properties and were formerly used medicinally; *bhang* (marijuana), *ganja*, and *charas* (hashish) are different forms. There is a strong connection between the sadhus, or Hindu holy men, and the Rastafarian use of ganja. Similar to these saints, Rastas often smoke communally from a chalice, which is considered proper and even holy among the more conservative Rastas. This East Indian influence on the West Indies derives from the influx of cheap Indian labor following the abolition of slavery in the English colonies.

ghazal The *ghazal* is a poetic form consisting of couplets that share a rhyme and a refrain. Each line must share the same meter.

Etymologically, the word literally refers to "the mortal cry of a gazelle." The animal is called *ghizaal,* from which the English word "gazelle" stems, or *Kastori haran* (*haran* refers to deer) in Urdu. *Ghazals* are traditionally expressions of love, separation, and loneliness, for which the gazelle is an appropriate image. A *ghazal* can thus be understood as a poetic expression of both the pain of loss or separation and the beauty of love in spite of that pain. The form is ancient, originating in tenth-century Persian verse. It is derived from the Persian *qasida.* The structural requirements of the *ghazal* are more stringent than those of most poetic forms traditionally written in English. In its style and content, it is a genre that has proved capable of an extraordinary variety of expression around its central theme. It is considered by many to be one of the principal poetic forms that the Persian civilization offered the eastern Islamic world. The *ghazal* spread into South Asia in the twelfth century under the influence of the new Islamic sultanate courts and Sufi mystics.

gheraoed   *Gherao,* meaning "encirclement," is a word originally from Hindi and is a typically South Asian way of protest. Usually, a group of people would surround a politician or a government building until their demands are met or answers given. The past tense of the verb, *gheroaed,* is commonly used in English-language newspapers.

Goddess Laxami   The Hindu goddess of wealth. Among Hindus, an ideal daughter or daughter-in-law is supposed to represent Laxami and bring luck and prosperity to her new family. Lachchami is a rural, less educated version of the Sanskrit name Laxami.

gundagardi   Hooliganism.

Haat bahin-chod   Get lost, sister-fucker.

hadia   Country liquor made from fermented rice.

Hai-hai   Shame, shame!

han   Yeah; often used as interrogative.

harami ka pilla   "Son of a bastard." A common curse. Literally, "pup of a bastard," but used to mean "bloody bastard."

harmonium   A bellows keyboard similar to the American reed organ. Invented in Paris by Alexandre Debain in 1842 and brought to India by Europeans in the nineteenth century.

Hatt re   "Move away." Figuratively: "Nonsense!"

Hau, hai, I, ya, iha, hum   These are *stobhas,* or "sound symbols," taken from ancient Sama Veda.

Hey, Bhagwan!   Literally, "Oh God!," referring to the Infinite Divinity, as opposed to one of many local gods.

hijra   Eunuch. In India, eunuchs are traditionally considered auspicious during happy ceremonies such as marriage or birth, when the *hijras* come and sing and dance, expecting tips. Today these same *hijras* are regarded as a menace, and the word is derisively used to describe spineless or cowardly men.

Inqualab   A war cry of revolutionists.

Intermediate exam   A final examination at the end of eleven years of schooling, roughly equivalent to high school. This exam has been largely abandoned in the modern Indian education system.

jaddoos   An Indian sweet, traditionally offered in Hanuman temples by devotees.

jal-tarang   A water-bowl xylophone (musical instrument). A set of glass bowls of different sizes are arranged in a row and filled with water. They produce musical notes when struck.

jhapad   An openhanded slap.

Joy Bojorong Boli!   Literally, "Long live Hanuman!" Hanuman is a god described in the four-thousand-year-old Hindu epic *Ramayana,* also called "Bojorang Boli" in the Bengali pronunciation of the Sanskrit Bajarang Bali.

kaka   Paternal uncle. Interchangeable with *kaku* as a term of endearment.

kathakali   An ancient Indian classical dance from Kerela, in south India, in which the dancers wear elaborate and colorful masks. These masks or their miniatures are used as wall decorations.

Khayali pulav, Madho buddhu   Translates approximately as "You are building castles in the air, stupid Madho."

kurta   A loose long shirt worn with pajamas. Popular summer wear.

La Marts, Calcutta   A popular nickname for the La Martinier School, one of the oldest and most prestigious schools in India, with campuses in Calcutta, Lucknow, and Lyon, France, and famous for its history and alumni. The only school in the world whose pupils have been awarded battle honors, in their defense of Lucknow Residency in 1857. Because of his schooling at La Marts,

Bibhash is intellectually sophisticated and understands Karna's reference to Little Red Riding Hood, while Pandey*ji* does not.

lakh   A hundred thousand rupees (one *lakh* in Indian currency is equal to about twenty-five hundred U.S. dollars)

lathi   Cane/stick.

Maafi   Literally, "pardon me."

mader-chods   Motherfucker.

Mahila Jagaran Manch   Women's empowerment forum.

Mahila Jagaran Morcha   Women Awakening Front, a generic name used by several feminist groups. It is a variation of Mahila Jagaran Manch, explained above. The terms *morcha* and *manch* are interchangeable.

Main mast! Han-han mast!   Literally, "I am on high!" A memorable line from the "sexy" song in the popular Hindi movie *Mast,* which means "having fun" or "excited." The title of the film has sexual connotations; an elephant in heat is supposed to be "mast."

Mannat in the *Hanuman mandir Mannat*   making a wish. *Hanuman:* a popular god of the Hindu pantheon. *Mandir:* Hindu temple.

masjid   Mosque.

masti   Fun.

maulvi sahib   A Muslim priest or teacher.

mazdoor   Laborer.

mera buddhu   Figuratively, "my silly man."

naaths   A slower variation of *quawwalis.*

nasbandi   Vasectomy.

neem Azadirachta indica.   An evergreen tree that reaches an average height of twenty meters and has many medicinal properties. In India, *neem* trees are thought to be the abodes of ghosts and ghouls.

neta-log   Political leaders.

O mera jaanu   Literally, "Oh, my love."

palki   Palanquin.

patwari   Village-level government official.

Peechche   Literally, "Get back!"

phokusbaji   Derived from "focus." This term is used colloquially in eastern India to denote gimmickry.

pik   A reddish stream of spit frequently squirted by tobacco *pan* eaters. *Pan* is betel leaf, often chewed with tobacco. The saliva is not swallowed but spit out, much like with a wad of tobacco.

pir   A Sufi saint.

quawwalis   Devotional songs of Muslims of Indian subcontinent. The lyrics are inspired by Sufi thoughts. *Sufism* is a mystic tradition within Islam and encompasses a diverse range of beliefs and practices dedicated to divine love and the cultivation of the heart.

Ranjish hi sahi, dil hi dukhane ke liye aa. / Aa fir se mujhe chchod ke jaane ke liye aa . . .   These are the opening lines of a famous Urdu *ghazal* written by Ahmad Faraz. The lyrics, with translation (adapted from the Internet):

> *Ranjish hi sahi, dil hi dukhane ke liye aa*
> Even if you have grievances, just come to torment my heart
> *Aa fir say mujhe chchod ke jaane ke liye aa*
> Come once again, even if only to leave me

Ravana   The evil ten-headed king from the epic *Ramayana*.

R/T handset   A police abbreviation for receiver/transmitter.

saale   Bloody; a variation of *sala* and *shaala,* in glossary.

saar   Sir. This is a localized accent of the English word in some eastern provinces.

sahib   *Sahib* is a Hindi and Bengali term of respect meaning sir, master, or lord. It comes from the Arabic *sahib,* originally "friend, companion" (derived from *sahiba,* meaning "he accompanied"). Its feminine form is *sahiba.* It was also used as respectful address for Europeans (first mention in 1673) as honored guests. Under the British raj, it became the customary form of address for a white "master" (*memsahib* being the female form) used by the ever polite, often (forcibly) servile natives. In modern India it is loosely used as the equivalent of "sir."

sala ganjedi   Bloody drug addict.

Shaitani   Evil. *Shaitan* is the Indo-Muslim term for Satan.

shaala haaramzada   Bengali pronunciation of *saala haramzada,* meaning "bloody bastard."

Shri   Sanskrit title of veneration for men. An Indian/Hindu honorific stemming from the Vedic conception of prosperity. Akin to "mister."

sirdar   Literally, "captain," but in the Indian coal mining industry, a designation used for labor supervisors.

tikka   *Tikka* with a soft initial *t* means a piece of meat, such as a cutlet. The popular dish chicken *tikka* is made of chicken cutlets in marinade. A Westernized version, chicken *tikka masala,* is a popular dish in the U.S. and the U.K.

thana   Local police station.

Trahi mam!   Literally, "save me/protect me." A Vedic chant used at the time of cremation; an appeal to God from the bereaved on behalf of the departing soul.

tulsi baba   *Tulsi* is the Sanskrit term for "basil." *Baba* is a holy man.

Unstarred parliament question   Indian members of parliament (MPs), the people's representatives, keep a check on the government by raising questions in the parliament to the concerned union minister. Questions come in two forms: starred and unstarred. Unstarred question are of lower significance and simply require a written reply to the MPs. Starred questions are considered important and require the minister to read out the official reply and answer up to twenty related questions spontaneously. For this he must be fully prepared.

Veer Hanuman   Literally, "Brave Hanuman!" Hanuman is a god described in the four-thousand-year-old Hindu epic *Ramayana*. He is presented as a humanoid ape and served as one of the bravest and most loyal warrior chiefs of Lord Rama. The most common depiction of Hanuman has him striking a pose with one foot on a rock, carrying a mountain in one palm and a war mace in the other. The story of Ramayana is similar to *The Iliad*: Rama's wife is abducted by a ten-headed devil (Ravana), and Hanuman plays an important role in the war that follows.

washery   A coal beneficiation plant where low-grade coal is "cleaned" by washing off impurities with the help of certain chemicals mixed in water.

Yama   The Hindu god of death. Like the Grim Reaper, Yama is represented as an old man with the scythe but also carries a rope with which to capture souls.